D0070514

WITHDRAWN

the
language
inside

WITHDRAWN

Also by Holly Thompson
Orchards

Thompson, Holly.
The language inside /
c2013.
33305227984741
mh   05/23/13

SON

the language inside

Delacorte Press

This is a work of fiction. Names, characters, places, and incidents either are the product of the author's imagination or are used fictitiously. Any resemblance to actual persons, living or dead, events, or locales is entirely coincidental.

Text copyright © 2013 by Holly Thompson
Front jacket photograph copyright © 2013 by Mark Owen/Trevillion Images
Back jacket and chapter opener photograph copyright © 2013 by Jules Kitano

All rights reserved. Published in the United States by Delacorte Press, an imprint of Random House Children's Books, a division of Random House, Inc., New York.

Delacorte Press is a registered trademark and the colophon is a trademark of Random House, Inc.

Visit us on the Web! randomhouse.com/teens

Educators and librarians, for a variety of teaching tools, visit us at
RHTeachersLibrarians.com

Library of Congress Cataloging-in-Publication Data
Thompson, Holly.
  The language inside / Holly Thompson. — 1st ed.
      p. cm.
  Summary: Raised in Japan, American-born tenth-grader Emma is disconcerted by a move to Massachusetts for her mother's breast cancer treatment, because half of Emma's heart remains with her friends recovering from the tsunami.
    ISBN 978-0-385-73979-5 (hc) — ISBN 978-0-375-89835-8 (ebook)
  [1. Novels in verse.   2. Moving, Household—Fiction.   3. Interpersonal relations—Fiction.
4. Breast cancer—Fiction.   5. Family life—Massachusetts—Fiction.   6. Tsunamis—Fiction.
7. Massachusetts—Fiction.   8. Japan—Fiction.]   I. Title.
  PZ7.5.T45Lan2013
  [Fic]—dc23
                                2012030596

The text of this book is set in 11.5-point Goudy.

Printed in the United States of America

10 9 8 7 6 5 4 3 2 1

First Edition

Random House Children's Books supports the First Amendment
and celebrates the right to read.

For Bob, Dexter and especially Isabel

Chapter 1

Aura

third time it happens
I'm crossing the bridge
over a brown-green race of water
that slides through town
on my way to a long-term care center
to start volunteering

pausing
to get my courage up

peering over a rail
by a
   Tow Zone
  No Stopping
   on Bridge
sign
glimpsing shadows
below the river's surface . . .

but when I look up
the sign is halved—
one side blank
the other saying
    Zone
    pping
    idge

I glance back at the water
that my grandma YiaYia says used to
power this town's mills
which are now closed or reborn
as outlet malls, doctors' offices
dance and art studios, clinics
and care centers like the one
I'm headed to
to work with a woman
who can't move her legs
her arms
her head
and can't even talk

but the water has a spot of darkness
and my blindness grows
to a black hole
and I begin
to panic

should I find this guy Sam
the other volunteer
from my high school
who'll introduce me
to the recreational therapy director?

should I return to the bus stop
and try to get to YiaYia's house?

I haven't lived here long
I don't have a cell phone yet
I don't know if there's a bus
to my grandmother's neighborhood
and I have just twenty minutes
before my speech and thoughts
                              shatter

I go for Sam

I cross the bridge
turn right then left
walk up the paved pathway to
the Newall Center for Long Term Care
where standing by the entrance
is a guy whose face looks
        half there
who says
I'm Sam Nang—you Emma?

I turn my head
pan his face with the half
of my vision that remains—
        Asian, I realize
        Japanese, I dare hope
        though I know that's doubtful
        here in Massachusetts

I tell him *yeah, but I'm sick*

when he gets that I mean it
he says *the lobby* . . .
and leads me inside to a waiting area
where I drop onto a chair

I feel in my bag
pull pills from a plastic case
and swallow two caplets with
the last swig of water
from my bottle

along the edge
of my blindness
flickers a crescent
of tiny triangles—
                white
                        edged by
                                cuts of blue
                        black
                yellow

my stomach turns
I close my eyes
try to slow my breathing
and feel the thud of Sam
sitting down beside me

I squint my eyes open
shade them with my hand
against too-bright lights
and tell him
my head
I can't see
I need to go home

      zigzags of light seem to
      bolt from his jaw

I tell him YiaYia's address
and phone number
I tell him
to tell her
migraine

he tries calling
but there's no answer

now I'm breathing too fast
and as the numbness
starts creeping up my arm
I can't help crying

okay, okay Sam says
I'll call Chris
he'll drive you home

I unwrap the scarf from around my neck
drape it over my head to hide in the dimness
wishing my grandmother had a cell phone she actually used
wishing my mother or father could come get me
wishing we'd never left Japan

under the scarf I let myself cry
missing my friends
from Kamakura
      Madoka, Kako, Kenji, Shin
from Yokohama
      Min, Grace, Yuta, Sophia
whispering their names
like a prayer
to get me out of here
a prayer to get me back there
where I know people
where I know my way around
where I know what to expect
where my body didn't do this

Sam speaks softly
into his phone
stows it
then goes off
and has a conversation
I can't quite hear
with a person
I can't quite see

when he comes back he's silent
just the lobby noise
surrounds us

after a while I feel him rise
return
and press a tissue
into my hand

I wipe my eyes
try to keep calm
try to keep the light out
just breathing
through the weave of the scarf
as we wait

finally Sam tugs my jacket
takes my arm
and leads me outside to a car
parked near the entrance

he speaks to the driver
          pain slams my head
I can hear words
          catch words

                    grandmother
          ride   *back*   *leap*
                sock   *close*
                    here

but I can't connect the words
to make meaning

I start to get in the car
get out
throw up in some bushes
wipe my mouth with
another tissue from Sam
get in the car
lie down on the backseat
my head covered with my scarf
and a towel the driver hands me

then I close my eyes
and let myself be driven off
to who knows where
by two guys—
> one I've just met
> one I don't know
> at all

when the car stops
        doors open
close
        open
close

the crescent of triangles
        pulses
        pulses
        pulses
my arm's numb
half my face, too
my head bowling-ball heavy

I hear talk
outside the window
hear the driver say *sleep*
then it's quiet

and I do

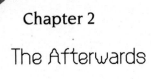

Chapter 2

The Afterwards

when I wake
it's dusk

I lie not moving
on the car seat
turn onto my back
and wait

sit up

wait

testing my head
my vision

the car has been pulled
into YiaYia's driveway
her back porch light is on

when I'm sure the worst
is really over
I get out
walk gingerly to the house
taking soft
      unjarring
           steps

from the porch I can see
my grandmother, the man and Sam
all seated in the living room around
the coffee table with emptied glasses
and a plate of rice cracker packets
that my father brought for Toby and me
his last visit from New York

at the kitchen sink
I rinse my mouth
wash my face
with paper towels
then join them
easing slowly into
one of YiaYia's armchairs

I'm Emma I say
resting my head
solidly on the chairback
nice to meet you

and everyone laughs

the man, Chris
Sam Nang's uncle
stands, says his wife
gets migraines, too

you taking anything for them? he asks
and I tell him the name of the pills
YiaYia's doctor gave me for
whenever the blindness hits

same as Beth he says

but I threw them up I say

that you did he says
and he and Sam smile

talk to Beth sometime Chris says
she'll tell you ways to avoid attacks—
sleep patterns, exercise . . .
it's good you slept
that's best

soon they're leaving
but I can't rise from where
I'm curled in the armchair
my head all aching and fuzzy
and full of the afterwards

but now that I'm not half blind
I can see that Chris's clothes are
spattered with paint and stain
and I can see that Sam is
     lean
     muscled
     and Asian
but Chris is not

I'm curious
but say nothing
remembering those girls
in the first meeting for Model UN
how when I asked
    anyone here speak Japanese?
one rolled her eyes and said
    Asian doesn't mean Japanese, you know
and when I tried to say
    of course not, I know that
    I'm from Japan, is all . . .
another girl looked me up and down and said
    yeah, sure, white girl
then a guy across the room whispered
    Japan—I thought she was glowing!
and everyone laughed

YiaYia walks Chris and Sam to the door
thanks them, returns, says
well, never a dull moment!
as she lays a fleece blanket over me

I come home to drop the groceries off
before going to the Newall Center to pick you up
and I find those two lounging on the porch steps—
I thought they'd broken in!
turns out they'd been sitting there
over an hour

they seem nice I say

yes she says
definitely your angels for today
I think I saw the boy
at the Newall Center once or twice
when I was there for your Papou

I ask
have you heard from Mom and Dad?
did Mom call?

YiaYia eyes me
I try to read her face
but I don't know
this grandmother well

we usually stay in Vermont
with Mom's mother and father
near our cousins up there
when we come back summers
not here with Dad's mother

YiaYia sizes up my state
        curled in the armchair
        fuzzy-headed
        recovering
then she picks up the empty glasses

did she call? I ask again

YiaYia puts down the glasses
comes to sit on the chair arm
leans close to me
and whispers
no, but I imagine she's doing just fine
so don't stress about it

I'm not stressing! I say
where's Toby?

she rises and arranges a basket
of patchwork coasters

 at a friend's for dinner

which doesn't seem fair
because right now
post-migraine
I just want someone
from my lived-in-Japan family

not YiaYia

who seems to think migraines can be controlled
just by flicking a brain switch
        some thoughts on
        some thoughts off

who wants me to be active and involved

who was the one to introduce me to
the Newall Center where my Papou
spent two years before he died

who when she heard they needed
a new volunteer poetry helper
piped right up with
my granddaughter writes poems!
meaning those verse scribbles
I'd write on her birthday cards

she thinks everything will be fine
if I just join groups

she thinks everything will be fine
if I just meet more Americans

and she thinks everything
will be fine in Japan
that it's better we're not there now
during the recovery

and she thinks
everything will be fine
in our family

but I think
she has a strange idea
of what's fine

I think she doesn't know
how much it hurt to leave
how much it felt like
abandoning Japan

and I think she doesn't know
how strange it is to live
without our father

and I think she doesn't
know what my mother is feeling
about having her breast lopped off

and I think she doesn't
know what it's like to be the daughter
wondering *do I carry those genes, too?*

my migraines started
three days after our move

my mother says I need
a strict routine

YiaYia sews me a lavender pillow
and says to avoid chocolate

my father emails me articles
one of an exhibit of paintings
by migraine sufferers that show
the dark hole of blindness
and the crescent
            of zigzagging
                        triangles
            just like mine

Toby doesn't say anything
after my migraines
just asks if I want a bath
to feel like I'm home in Japan

but Toby's not here now
so in the armchair I
pull the scarf over my head
and hide inside

YiaYia sighs
pats my arm
picks up the glasses
and goes into the kitchen

Chapter 3

Gone

I was at the international school
where I'd transferred for grade 9
        from Japanese school
I was in English class
when it started
        a tremor
                        that grew

Mr. Hays had taught in Japan
only two years so I shouted at him
and at Ryan and Keizo
who were playing tough
"surfing" the quake
get under the desks!
this isn't normal!

the building rattled
shelves, books, cupboards clattered
stuff crashed and fell

I thought the walls would give
I thought the windows would shatter
and I was glad
I'd worn my boots
they'd keep me warm
if the school collapsed

on and on
the building
bumped
creaked
swayed
clanked

while under the desks
we clutched hands
Sophia on one side of me
Yohei on the other

with the principal's voice on the loudspeaker
now it's slowing, wait, here's another tremble
stay calm, stay calm, it will be over soon
but it seemed like forever

later as we waited
in our classrooms
aftershocks jolting

power came on
network was up
but cell phones
were down

from a school computer
I blast-emailed Mom, Dad, Toby, Madoka
YiaYia, Gram, Gramps, cousins—
big quake, I'm at school, everyone here okay
not knowing who would see my message
or when

trains were stopped
people were stuck
I couldn't get back to Kamakura
and finally was dismissed
to walk with Juulia to her house

where I translated Japanese TV news
for them while her mother followed
Finnish and English news online

and where we watched in disbelief
as tsunami waves engulfed
the Pacific coast of Tohoku

I tried calling Madoka in Kamakura
whose grandparents, cousins
aunts and uncles
all live up north in Miyagi
near the sea

I sat on Juulia's sofa
stone still
holding my head
hoping those relatives had all
                              run
                                        fast

near midnight I reached
Mom and Toby in Kamakura
      their power and heat finally on
      Dad staying the night in Tokyo
and right away I asked
but Mom said no
Madoka's family
hadn't heard any news

seeing those waves blast away
seaside towns that looked like ours
towns that could have been ours
towns I've visited
with Madoka . . .

I hardly slept
all night

I rose
when I finally heard
someone else up at dawn
and joined Juulia's father
in stunned silence
in front of the TV

midday on the day after
Mom came by car to get me

and back in Kamakura
I went straight to Madoka's house

to help them try to make contact
to help them wait for news

Dad got home that second night
by train, bus, walking

and on the third day we learned
that Madoka's grandparents

survived
her cousins were safe

but later we learned
the first floor of her grandparents' house
was ruined
one cousin's school
was gone
one uncle's fishing boat
was gone
one uncle's factory
was gone
one aunt's sister
was gone
one uncle's wife
was gone
and the list
of gone
went on
and on

Chapter 4

Cleanup

in late April, Dad and I
Madoka and her father
packed a van full of supplies
cleanup gear and two used bicycles
and drove north to Miyagi

at her grandparents' house
the waterline
was above my head

a car stood on its nose
between the kitchen wall
and a neighbor's wall

another had bashed down a shed
and four were crumpled
against a broken utility pole

the garden was littered
with splintered chairs, a drum
shredded mats, plastic crates, clothes
a urinal and dresser drawers

trees crusted with mud
were hung with trash
tangled in string
and weighted with dead fish

Madoka's Jiichan, her grandfather
pried open the door to his house
and we peered inside to furniture
heaped, overturned
reeking and stuck
in oily salty sludge

but at least they still had a house—

a couple streets away
the waterline hit two stories
and beyond that
all the way to the sea . . .

there was only rubble

we dressed in rainsuits and boots
helmets, masks and goggles
and worked our way inside
shoveling muck into bags
lugging bags out

Madoka and I were a team
taking turns bag-holding
muck-shoveling
picking out rotting fish
removing broken glass

teams of men hauled out
soaked tatami mats
and ruined appliances

we shoveled sludge from floors
then from under floors
from behind the toilet
from inside kitchen cabinets

we salvaged
      dishes, pots and pans
      jewelry, photos, unopened bottles of sake

we discarded
      furniture, futons, clothes, books, shoes, papers
      phones, place mats, curtains, stuffed animals

during lunch or breaks
sometimes Madoka and I
wandered the deserted neighborhood
among growing mounds of debris

we'd greet
whoever we saw
stop to talk
offer help

or just listen

once we found two girls
leaping onto and off
bent and broken
washed-up cars
wearing

      no gloves
      no masks
      no boots
so Madoka and I led them away
to a cleared patch of asphalt
found some stones
and started hopscotch

first the long spiral snaking kind
we learned in Japanese preschool

then the kind like a double-crossed T
I learned in Vermont

at night
in the tent we'd pitched
in a little park on high ground
I wrote by lantern light
some of the words people said to us

and some of the things
I couldn't believe
we'd seen

we worked dawn to dusk
and on the fourth day
Madoka's grandmother
came from the evacuation center
to view the house
and the changed neighborhood

stoic, tough
she'd come to join the cleanup

but when she saw my yellow rainsuit
greasy with sludge
my gloves foul black

she fell against my shoulder
and wept
even you, Emma-chan
even you are here to help

in June Mom and I returned for a week
to help Madoka's cousins
and her grandparents' neighbors
still shoveling
still cleaning
still bagging
and heaping debris

and in August I went up with Madoka
for what should have been two weeks
of helping all around
her grandparents' town . . .

and that's where I was
when I got the news

about Mom

about our move
out of Japan

Chapter 5

The Next Minute

I had to leave Miyagi
return early to Kamakura
help with packing, sorting, storing

could only drop by
        the international school
        as classes were starting
could only drop by
        a volleyball practice
        at my old Japanese school
to say my good-byes

one minute my head was full of tsunami cleanup
with plans to visit Miyagi each school break

one minute I was a member of student council
with fund-raising plans for two adopted Tohoku schools

one minute I was headed back to teachers who knew me
a coach eyeing me for varsity volleyball
and a Model UN conference in the Philippines

one minute Toby was finishing summer homework
for his second term at Japanese middle school
after all-summer practice with his baseball club

one minute we thought the earthquake
was the only thing
to turn our lives upside down this year

but the next minute
Mom's mammogram
changed everything

the next minute
she'd gone back to the U.S.
for biopsies and MRIs

the next minute
she'd scheduled surgery
for September in Boston

the next minute
I was saying good-bye to
my school
our Kamakura home
our neighborhood
our cat Shoga
my new friends
my old friends
Madoka

and nearly the next minute
I was starting tenth grade
in a country I'd lived in only as a baby
in a state I'd never lived in
in my father's mother's town

without my father
without any friends
who speak Japanese
or know anything about Japan
except sushi, manga, anime
tsunami and radiation

and my mother
getting poked and sliced
and rearranged

Dad's now based
at the firm's New York branch
joining us here in Massachusetts
for appointments and procedures
then rushing back to work in Manhattan
while we remain in YiaYia's town
where we came to live
in time for Mom's first surgery

which then revealed
the whole breast had to go

this week my mother went down to visit my father
a getaway before the full mastectomy
her trip is only five days
but already it feels like weeks

I miss her
I miss Dad
I miss Madoka
I miss Japan

my heart is torn in two—
half here with Mom
and all she's going through
half there in Japan
with Madoka
and her relatives
all coping
with so much gone

Chapter 6

Beads

Saturday afternoon in YiaYia's kitchen
Toby and I paint clay beads with tiny brushes

YiaYia wants us to decorate a bead each for Mom
for some necklace idea she has in mind

she's even figured out how to put the bead
on a wire stretched between two cup handles
so we can turn it and paint all sides

just go ahead, try something
YiaYia urges
there are plenty of beads she says

she bought extras
so we can make mistakes

I'm trying to think of
some simple kanji character
suitable for a single bead
that's clearly way too small
for the four-character proverb
I'd thought I'd try

finally I settle on the characters
for *genki*

元気

meaning health or energy

and even though they are easy
grade-school kanji
it takes me three tries to get the *ki* right
on the curve of the bead
and I'm glad that YiaYia
bought extras

Toby sees mine and tries the kanji
for *katsu*

勝

victory
but on that small bead
the strokes are too hard
so he gives up and changes
to the character
for *chikara*

力

strength

watching him I think of
the day Mom, Toby and I left Kamakura
when Madoka came to say good-bye
with her mother who gave

my mother
        an amulet from Hachiman Shrine
        with a gold crane for long life
me
        a cell-phone strap
        with a dove and ginkgo leaf

and Toby
        a tiny arrow
        like the one Yoritomo launched at evil spirits
        and a sports towel
        with the character for *katsu*

they waved and waved
as we pulled out of the driveway
and turned down the lane
pressing handkerchiefs to their eyes
calling *itte irrashai!*—go and return!

which is what you say
for an ordinary everyday farewell
when you send someone off
for school or work

when you expect them to go and return

and we replied, even though
we were moving for who knows how long
      six months?
      a year?
      forever?
itte kimasu—we'll go and return

Dad drove us to Narita
then worked in Tokyo two more weeks
before moving to New York
and driving up to Boston
for the first surgery

some days I want him to quit the firm
find a new job in Boston
so he can commute from YiaYia's house
and be here with us all the time

but most days I want him to work hard
stay in New York
do whatever it is he needs to do
to stay with that firm

which is our ticket out of America
and back to Japan when Mom is better

I check our beads drying
      genki, chikara
      health, strength
and I think
please

Chapter 7

Seawall

this town of YiaYia's is in the woods
on a river that flows somewhere
eventually into the sea
but there's no sea
anywhere in sight

here in YiaYia's town
I can walk and walk
in any direction
but I never see
or smell
the sea

from our house
in Kamakura
it's a ten-minute walk
or five-minute run to the beach
and at the eastern end of town
the beach meets a headland
and there's a lane to take you out
around the headland
to a marina
with tall palms
and condominiums
and views of the bay
Enoshima
Izu Peninsula
Mount Fuji

I go there in winter when the air is cool
and the sun off the sea warms the wall
or in summer when the air is hot
but the breeze off the water blows cool

my mother always ran
from home to the marina
then from eastern headland
to western headland
and from western headland
back home again

she says she kept her health
all these years
running by the sea
       lungs full of seaweed air
       tropical breezes
       cold gusts
       typhoon winds

now standing here in YiaYia's backyard
bordering other backyards
that border more houses and woods
I would love to fill my lungs
with damp seaweed air

after I left Miyagi
when I learned of Mom's decision
to have the surgery in the States
and Dad's decision for us
to attend school in Massachusetts
I called Shin, my close friend
from middle school

meet me at the beach I said
I need to talk

he did
and we walked to the center
of the beach curve
where the river enters the bay
then back to the eastern headland
by the windsurfers

and when the beach ran out
we continued into the marina
all the while
not talking

the marina seawall is long and high
and you're not supposed to climb it
or sit on it but everyone does

you have to run at the wall
and keep running when you hit the wall
to gain enough height to haul yourself up
to the top

I skinned my knee
and as we sat between people casting for fish
and I told Shin the news
we watched a trickle of blood
track down my leg
turn toward my calf
then stop
and dry

I don't know what will happen
what all this means I said

and he put his arm around me
and I leaned into him
one of my oldest best friends

as the coppery coin of sun
slid into the haze

but then as if he hadn't heard
a word of what I'd been saying—
      my mother, cancer, moving to America
he said *itsuka kokutte ageyo ka na*—
      one day I might tell you I love you

and I pulled away
and stared at him

what?

maybe, in the future
he said, and smiled
like I'd be grateful

and I said
why are you saying that?
why now?
did you hear a word I told you?
baka!—jerk!
and I smacked him
on the back of his head

then I started to cry
I hadn't meant to hit him

he said he was sorry
and held his head down
and I shook my head, said
it's not you

I put his arm back around me
and leaned into him
but he looked away
toward the pinking sky

finally I licked my fingers
washed the track of blood
from my leg and we walked
back to my house not talking

just before we got there
I told him again I was sorry
in the future if you tell me you love me
I promise not to hit you

we both tried to smile
he said *don't forget me*
and I promised I wouldn't

then we nodded
and finger-waved
good-bye

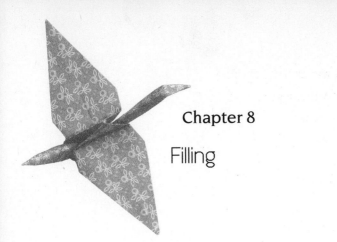

Chapter 8

Filling

I have to wait a whole week
till my next Wednesday visit
at the Newall Center for Long Term Care

I look for Sam Nang at my new school
big as a college campus
with over 1,200 students
so many classes and different levels
and kids tall and loud
but in the crowds I never see him
and I realize I don't even know
which grade he's in

I hardly know anyone at this school
just some kids in my classes
and the Model UN team—
since I missed tryouts
for soccer and volleyball
         and just my luck
         both my sports
         here in Massachusetts
         are fall sports

I'm trying dance club
even though they dance at pep rallies
and halftime shows
and so far this fall
I'm not so full of pep

but Tracy, the captain
seems glad to have me
says I have awesome flexibility
says *good, good, that's it*
as I try following
their routines

after classes most days I go home
on the school bus
missing Japan's fast trains
freedom

at YiaYia's
I listen to the same old songs
play with the new cell phone
that Toby and I now share
do homework on Mom's laptop
research Venezuela for Model UN
           Chavez and petroleum
           health care and politics
but soon I'm reading
news of Tohoku
and updates from friends in Japan
making comments on posts hours old
feeling time-warped and remote

I friend the few people I've met here
search for Sam Nang
but I don't find any Sam Nangs
who look at all like Sam Nang

when Mom returns
from New York
she manages and directs us
> the way to slice the sandwiches
> which dressing for the salad
> the proper way to dry the plates
> what homework to do first
> how to fold our laundry
and we all turn quiet
just following orders
till she gets it out of her system

YiaYia takes me aside
tells me not to talk back
just let her be she says
she needs to feel in charge

obliging, Toby and I move furniture into
and out of our grandmother's den
to make a bedroom on the first floor
where Mom will soon recover

I want to talk with Madoka
but she's only online
when I'm home weekends
during her late evening
which is my late morning

Madoka's mother insists we write letters
and since it's through Madoka and her mother
that my Japanese is what it is
          native level with no accent
once a week I handwrite
a proper letter
          starting with a seasonal comment
          asking after Madoka's relatives
          sharing bits of news
          and inquiring about hers

I treat it like an assignment
that I want to do well
and add an extra page
for her grandparents
or cousins in Tohoku

but I miss just being with Madoka
with Madoka I could always talk
                              or not talk
either way she understood

like before we left Japan
when Madoka and I went to the beach
to swim before dinner

it wasn't very clean
never is late August
but Madoka's head bobbed on the waves
the cliffs rose in the distance
and above them, nearly not there
the faint gray stamp of Mount Fuji

when a plastic bag
turned into a jellyfish
we scrambled out, showered
then walked to the end of the beach
where the windsurfers go in
and where the rocks of an ancient
artificial island
surface at low tide

we waded through shallows
over rippled sand
staring at those rocks
heaped hundreds of years ago
to make the safe harbor
we'd studied in school

and as we stared at that history
which I'd come to think of as mine
Madoka said softly

amerika-jin ni nacchau—
        you'll turn into an American

I am *an American* I said

but inside you're Japanese Madoka said
using the word *nakami*—filling
for inside

I laughed
said *well, that won't change*

good Madoka said
and don't start talking all loud and obnoxious
or eating too much

I won't! I said

don't change she said
then I noticed
her chin trembling

we wandered back from the sandbar
and when we reached dry beach
she stopped

remember when we first went up to Miyagi
after the tsunami?
I nodded

and we first looked into Jiichan
and Baachan's house?
I nodded

I didn't think I could do it
I thought I'd made a mistake
going there so soon after
and with my aunt still missing
but you just grabbed one of the shovels
handed me a bag and started in on the mud
bag by bag, you said
you'd read that on someone's blog
that's how to get it done
and you were right, bag by bag

she looked at me sideways
then turned back to the waves
they'll be waiting for you up there, you know
all of my relatives

I whispered
it might be a year
sick at the thought
I could be away that long
or longer

she nodded
that's okay
they'll still be waiting

her eyes glistened
and I knew that it wasn't so much for our parting
as for all that had happened this year
all we'd seen together
        smashed cars
        fish in trees
        sad eyes of people
        and debris we'd bagged and added
        to heaps upon heaps of debris
        in an endless stretch of ruined towns

I stood with her on the wet sand
this friend I'd walked to elementary and
middle school with
    took ballet with
        played volleyball with

this friend whose grandmother's arms
    we'd held as we searched the rubble
        of her missing daughter-in-law's home

we didn't need words
we just inhaled and exhaled
side by side
watching the waves

until she said
we'll weigh you
before and after

what?

she smirked
to see if you get fat

she was good at that
reading the air
saying the right thing
at the right moment
moving us along
back to joking

I gave her a shove
we walked up the shore
unlocked our bicycles
and rode back to her house
to eat our last two-family meal together—
for how long? I knew we all wondered

at this school in Massachusetts
I listen to clips of conversations
move from class to class
biology to art to English to Chinese
wondering who of these 1,200 students I should talk to
and how I can begin conversations
or try to make friends
with my filling
so different from theirs

I don't know when to say what
I don't know if something's funny or not
I don't get sarcasm
layered over sarcasm
and jokes made by
unjoking faces

I know how to read silence in Japan
I can read the air in Japan
but I don't have a clue
how to read the air here

Chapter 9

Patients

by Wednesday I'm so glad
to get on a bus to the Newall Center
grateful to go someplace different
from school and YiaYia's house

on the bridge over the river
I check the No Stopping sign
in case of blindness—
but auras never seem to happen
when you're ready

Sam is there
by the entrance
just like last week
and he stares at me
checking, it seems
to see if I'm okay

it's nice
to be able to see all of him
this time

where to? I say
and he smiles, leads me inside
where we sign in at the main desk
go down a corridor
up an elevator onto a ward
to a nurses' station

this is the new volunteer
Emma . . .
Sam says and looks at me

Karas
I say
then spell it

I hand in my doctor's report
results of my TB test
permission slip from my mother
and receive an ID card
to hang around my neck

soon we're following a woman named Lin
who says she's the rec director
who helps the poet who runs the writing program
the poet who comes from the university
for a workshop once a month
the workshop that patients
        participate in
that we, too, are encouraged
        to participate in
if we can

Lin says she also runs the music and art programs
even some dance because
that's what a rec director does

she makes a joke about the wrecks she directs
and she and Sam are laughing
but it takes me a while to catch on

she and Sam chat
as we walk through the ward
he says something about a Mr. Sock
and I swear she then asks about Mr. Shoe
and then they go on about a Mr. Pen
and Mr. Pencil
and it's like they're speaking
another language
even though the words
are English

all the while I'm looking around the ward
checking to see if I'll be able to handle this
      tubes and needles stress me
      I have to lie down
      when I get shots

but so far
as I follow Sam and Lin
down corridors
peeking into rooms
I'm not seeing people hooked up
to lots of tubes

finally we stop at room 427
and Sam steps inside ahead of Lin
and puts his hands together to greet two men
      one in a bed
      one in a chair
and this time
I know it's not English
that I'm not understanding
and I look at the names on the wall—
      Leap Sok
      and Chea Pen

Sam Nang's patient, Leap Sok
Lin says gesturing
and that's Chea Pen
who sometimes joins in
and now Pen sounds like Pine

Sam Nang works with them
in Khmer and English
she adds

then she turns
to lead me away
from the men
from Sam

wait!
I say

and Sam looks at me
and Lin looks at me
the two men look at me
and I feel my face
heat up

can I talk to you? I say
looking straight at Sam
ask you some questions?
at the end, I mean?

and Sam nods
sure, I'll come by Zena's room at 5:00

Zena's room? I say

your patient he says
and Lin leads me
away from Sam
and we are off

Chapter 10

S-e-x-y M-a-n

we go down another hall
and Lin is saying
Zena's a sweetie
she's got spunk, too
you'll love working with her

when her eyes go up, that's yes
that's all you have to know
oh, and that a slash means
the end of a line in a poem

usually she's in her chair
but that's being fixed today

and then we're outside
room 448
I take a deep breath
and in we go

she is just a head propped up on a pillow
the rest of her hidden beneath
covers, her graying hair
brushed back and clipped
with purple barrettes on either side

her eyes follow me
and seem to smile

Lin says
Zena Hickox
this is Emma Karas
who will help you write
your masterpieces

and Zena's eyes look up

Lin shows me the letter board, says
there's more sophisticated equipment
computers that track eye movement
but until an angel comes along
to help us fund such a system
this is what we have

she holds up a piece of laminated paper
with the alphabet in five rows
each row colored different
>
> red, yellow, blue, green, purple
> and in the last row—orange—
> small words, question words
> numbers, symbols

Lin shows me how to hold it up
and say the colors
then the letters of that row
watching for when Zena's eyes go up
to find which letter or small word
or symbol she means

and then I realize
I will be helping her write poems
letter by letter
and I start to panic

okay, honey? Lin says
and I want to say *no way!*
I want to say *I have to go*
this was a mistake
and I'm wishing YiaYia
had found me volunteer work
in a soup kitchen
or tutoring kids
or river cleanup
anything else . . .

but I nod

okay, Zena? Lin says
and Zena's eyes
go up

Lin walks out the door
and then it's just me and Zena
and the sounds of whatever she's
hooked up to
which I try not to look at
or think about
and I don't know what to say

I sit down on the chair by her bed
arrange my jacket over the chairback
set my pack on the floor
pull out a notebook and pen
open to a page of blank paper
take a deep breath
then glance at her

she looks up

I like your barrettes I say
her eyes roll up
and I'm relieved
but I don't know what else to say
to someone who can't talk

so I unzip my sweatshirt
and waste some time
arranging my sleeves

shall we start? I finally say
but she looks straight at me

I mean with a poem I add
still she doesn't look up
and I'm thinking I might need
to go get one of the aides

but then I try
you want to do something else?
and she looks up

I don't know what it is
so I pick up the letter board
and say the colors—*red, yellow* . . .
and run my fingers over the letters
of the row she selects
as I say them

i-n-t-r-o she spells
introduction? I ask
and Zena looks up
like self-introductions? I ask
and Zena looks up again

ah! I say, so relieved
to have figured out what she means
that I jump right in blabbing
that I grew up in Japan
and went to Japanese schools
then switched to international school last year
but had to move here to my grandmother's house
because of my mother's . . .
                                        breast

Zena's mouth goes wide
and she makes a throaty sound
and at first I think she's choking
or I've made an embarrassing mistake
but her eyes seem to smile
and I realize this growl is her laugh

I go on to explain the first surgery
and the second surgery coming up
and how we'll live here till Mom recovers
and maybe longer
we just don't know
and I say
but I miss Japan
like I'm missing a person

and I don't know why this is all coming
out of me because I never talk like this
to anyone

I say to Zena *now your turn*
but her eyes don't go up
I stare back at her
and she seems to gaze at the letter board
so I say the colors and letters
and she spells

e-a-r-t-h-q-u-
and I guess the end
and tell her about the quake
and tsunami
and Madoka's relatives
and the ongoing cleanup work

okay, now you I say
anxious to turn the conversation
to her but she stares at me
and spells
s-o s-o-r-r-y
and I nod
say *thanks*

when she continues to stare
I do the colors and letters again
and she spells
r u i-n l-o-v-e
and I can't believe she asked me that

I roll my eyes
say *no!*
and she makes that growl sound again

now you I say
this time firmly
a self-introduction!

I ask Zena questions
are you from Massachusetts?
her eyes go up
this town?
her eyes go up
maybe you knew my grandmother—
Elena Karas? Contos before she married . . .
Zena's eyes don't move
so I ask *how old are you?*
then flinch
sorry! that was rude

Zena looks at the letter board
chooses orange, the last row
where in one box it says *numbers*
so I count for her by tens, then ones
and discover she's 46
even though she looks
older than YiaYia
who's 71

I take off my sweatshirt
flushed and embarrassed
feeling like a total failure at this

is purple your favorite color? I ask
her eyes go up
will you dress up for Halloween? I ask
her eyes go up
as what? I ask
m-e-r-m-a-i-d she spells
and I laugh and tell her she'll be a great mermaid
and I'll help her with her costume

then I say *so, should I bring some poems*
to read next time before we write?
her eyes go up
I'm not sure what else to ask
but then I remember that question
she asked me
are you in love?

Zena looks up
and she growls
and she eyes the letter board
so I hold it up and she spells
s-e-x-y m-a-n
and I crack up
time to write poems! I say

so we start
and it is slow
this one-letter-at-a-time thing
I try guessing words partway through
but if I guess too soon Zena gets mad

once I guess
dryer? drugstore? dressing room?
before she's finished the word
then she starts again, spells
d-o-d-o
and glares
at me

I bow, apologize
start again
and follow her exactly
without rushing

and now we have a first line
which I realize is a line
because she chooses a slash:

   I open the door to my dreams

next line I say
but Zena doesn't look up
no? there's more for this line?
but still she doesn't look up

we go back to the letter board
and she spells *u*

you? I ask
you mean me?
her eyes go up
and then I get it
she wants us to take turns
so I say *okay,* read
   I open the door to my dreams
and add the line
   and see the face . . .

your turn I say
and slowly Zena spells
    of the one I love

and I see she is playing a game
trying to trap me
into revealing something personal

so I say
    gazing back at me
then she spells
    in fear
so I say
    and adoration

and then I hear someone behind me
and Sam is standing there
in the doorway
and I feel my face go hot
and Zena's eyes go up
and she growls

we're almost done
I say to Sam

he says *take your time*
and comes into the room
and leans on the windowsill

and I think by his broad shoulders there
outlined by the late-afternoon light
he must be a swimmer

Zena and I
go back and forth and at last
we've written

> I open the door to my dreams
> and see the face
> of the one I love
> gazing back at me
> in fear
> and adoration
> and wonder
> then I know
> this is the face
> of the one who is
> my daughter

and I'm surprised by her last line
expecting something instead about her
s-e-x-y m-a-n

I ask if we've finished the poem
but Zena doesn't look up
and I realize it's my turn

so I think
then add the line
> to be

Zena looks up
when I add that
but doesn't look up
when I ask
if she wants to keep going

Sam tells me
to read the whole thing
again

and I do

nice he says
and Zena looks up

by then it's nearly dark outside
so I tell Zena I'll see her next week
and I'll type this one up
for her notebook

Zena spells *t-h-a-n-k u*
and I say *there's a short way to do that*
and show her how to spell
39 for *sankyu*—
        san for three
        kyu for nine
which is how *thank you* sounds
with a Japanese accent

I put on my sweatshirt
tell her I'll bring poems
and we'll write
more masterpieces
and Zena
looks up again

Chapter 11

Ghosts

it's after five when we sign out at the nurses' station
tell them to tell Lin that we're leaving
head down the corridors
to the elevator
sign out in the lobby
and step outside
                    to the slap
of cold autumn air

Sam says that Chris is coming
they can give me a ride
and Chris already called YiaYia
to tell her she doesn't have to come
since my grandmother's house is
sort of on the way

we can wait over there Sam says
so we cross the bridge
over the darkened river
which we can't see
so much as smell
and which Sam says is
not a river
but a canal
from the mill days
and we stand in the red and green light
of a pizza sign

you live with your uncle—Chris? I say

and aunt he says

is that good? I ask *living with them?*

yeah, it's good
  and I wonder if he's adopted
  even though he calls them "uncle" and "aunt"
but before I can ask he says
how about you?
how's living with your grandmother?

and I say
it's okay
for now
that's all
because I just don't want to go into everything

and he says
I hear you

we're standing there
angled toward each other
with the neon pizza sign
splashing red and green swaths across his face
the smell of pizza reminding me I'm starved

and right now I don't want to go home yet
to my same old music
and my grandmother and brother
and my mother and her upcoming surgery

I just want to go inside this pizza place
and talk with this guy Sam
and pretend even briefly
that everything is normal

but Chris pulls up in the car
and Sam gets in the front
and I get in the back
and that's that

in the car we talk about Zena and how she called me a dodo
and when I tell them she spelled *s-e-x-y m-a-n*
they both crack up and Sam says he bets he knows who it is—
her sexy man

who? another patient? I ask

no he says *a poet guy*

I ask about Mr. Sok and Mr. Pen and
and Sam says that Leap Sok, who he calls
Lok Ta Leap—Grandfather Leap
is writing a memoir
but his hand doesn't work now
because of a stroke
and Lok Ta Chea is writing some letters
for his grandchildren and a little bit
about the refugee camp
but he hasn't been well lately

refugee camp? I ask

Sam says *yeah, in Thailand*
after he escaped Cambodia
when the Vietnamese
drove out Pol Pot

and from that one sentence
I realize that even though I'm good at geography
and even though I know those countries' capitals
I know hardly any Southeast Asian history
which seems unforgivable
having grown up in Japan

but I nod when Sam turns to look at me
nod thoughtfully as if I get it
and I promise myself
to learn something
before I see him next
to figure out
   what is this language Khmer
   that he and Mr. Sok and Mr. Pen speak

for now I say
that sounds tough

and Sam says *yeah, it can be*
some days I help them with English
things they don't know how to say to aides or nurses
most days Lok Ta Chea can't get out of bed
he can barely see and his feet are swollen
Lok Ta Leap is the one I work with more
and it's mostly his memories
of his village and his parents
and the temple he lived at
and the work he did later
and how he made it through Pol Pot times
and stories of his grandparents
and sometimes ghosts who do things
like break someone's neck
because the person did something bad

Sam is then silent

ghosts, I'm thinking from the backseat
and I'm reminded of a story that Shin once told
on a school trip to Kyoto

the story Shin told us in the dark when he and Kenji
    snuck into our room
was about students sleeping on the second floor of the inn
where our class was staying and how one student woke up
and saw a figure walking back and forth
past the room's window

at first the student didn't think anything of it
    and fell back asleep
but he woke again and saw the figure still going back and forth
so he thought someone was on the path outside the window
but then he remembered there was no path outside the window
so he thought someone was on the balcony outside the window
but then he remembered there was no balcony outside the window
and they were on the second floor

the student woke the others
who didn't see any figure
so the next night when it appeared again
he went outside to check
but never came back

now at the inn they say that sometimes guests
see the shadowy forms of two figures
walking back and forth
outside the windows

and if you go outside to check, who knows
maybe soon, there'll be three

I remember Shin sitting near me
and I start to think about him
and what he said on the seawall
and how I shouldn't have
called him *baka*

then to stop myself from thinking of Shin
I tell that ghost story
to Sam and Chris

Sam and Chris laugh when I finish
Chris says *good one!*
and suddenly we're at YiaYia's house
much sooner than I expected
and I feel like a fool for babbling
not asking more about Leap Sok and Chea Pen

at least I remember
to ask for Sam's cell-phone number
before getting out of the car

they back down the driveway
Sam rolls down his window
you sleep up there?
pointing to YiaYia's second story

I nod
he says *watch out!*
and I laugh

Chapter 12

Luck

the next day after school
I recall the bit Sam said
about the refugee camp in Thailand
and something about Cambodia and Vietnam
so I search on the Web

and read about
the killing fields

and how over a million Cambodians were killed
from 1975 to 1979
by execution and torture
by Cambodians led by Pol Pot

and how a million more died
of starvation and malnutrition
brought on by policies of forced labor
families uprooted
separated
moved around the country
digging ditches, building roads
cultivating crops with crude tools
made to toil and grow food
as they starved

educated city dwellers
teachers
doctors
artists
dancers
were all targets

you had to pretend to be a peasant
to have always been a farmer
to act illiterate
to keep silent
to hope
to survive

I learn that the Vietnamese invaded
and drove Pol Pot out of power
but there was famine and still more fighting

I learn that people fled to Thailand
lived in border camps
and eventually the lucky ones
were sent on to third countries
like the U.S.

I learn that Massachusetts took in refugees

I learn that Lowell is nearly
one-third Cambodian

I learn that Cambodians speak Khmer

and Khmer is pronounced *Khmai*
when it means the language

and I realize that Sam Nang must be
at least part Cambodian
and now I have a hundred questions
I want to ask him

a couple days later my mother borrows the DVD
The Killing Fields from the library
and one night after Toby and YiaYia
have gone to bed we keep the volume low
and she and I stay up and watch
the harrowing true story of Dith Pran
how he wasn't allowed to leave
how he tried to escape
and then was made a slave
laboring in the mud
how he survived by a mix
of luck and sharp wits

I almost wish we hadn't watched
it's so grim
and long past the end
and the haunting music
even after we have ejected the DVD
we sit there stunned

finally Mom says
well, I guess I can't feel sorry for myself
can I?

we tiptoe into the kitchen
to make *yuzu* citrus tea
from a big jar of preserves Mom bought
at a Korean market in New York

over the tangy aroma
as the tea is cooling
she whispers
we're lucky, Em—
even now
with my lousy breast

Chapter 13

Slipping

I know I'm losing my Japanese—
words aren't there
when I reach for them

and I have to check the dictionary
when I write letters to Madoka
even though I practice kanji
in the workbooks she sent me

I'm already behind Madoka
because I switched to international school
where the native-level Japanese classes
are a year behind the national curriculum
ninth grade was a review year for me
tenth was supposed to be new material at last

my goal was always just to keep up with her

now my goal is just to keep myself
from going backward

but without seeing kanji all around me
without hearing Japanese each day
without writing Japanese in class
I know I'm slipping

in YiaYia's kitchen
my mother's stirring soup
and telling me to stop worrying—
     my foundation in the language is solid
     we'll return eventually and
     I can study it again in university

you don't have to rely on Madoka or her mother she says
you can hire a tutor and take the proficiency tests
you can pick up and continue the language anytime
here or there

but I'm so on the verge I say

the verge of what? she asks

complete fluency I say
what I'd need to enter a Japanese university

I didn't know that's what you were thinking she says

I'm not necessarily
I don't know yet
but I want that option

then study she says
don't lose it
like it's as simple as that

Mom's not as fluent as I am
she doesn't know how hard it is
to hold on to those kanji you learn
and use in high school
if you're not surrounded by them

I sigh
loud

and that sigh seems to set her off
I don't have a magic wand, Em
to make everything just right
so here—
you stir

and she storms out

I apologize to her back
and to YiaYia
who's looking at me like
what was I thinking
and I stir the soup
until YiaYia turns it off
and tells me I can stop

she's so sensitive
I complain

I'll say Toby adds
she explodes at anything

well, of course she's sensitive!
YiaYia snaps
scowling at us both
so give her space
and hold your tongues

upstairs after sulking
about holding my tongue
and tiptoeing around Mom
I think some more
on what's strange
about being here
and I realize

it's not just losing
Japanese words
and phrases

it's as if I've lost
half of myself here
but no one knows
because I'm a *white girl*

here
I don't look like I belong in Japan
here
I don't look out of place
here
everyone thinks I must be glad
to be "back" in Massachusetts

as if this were home
        but it's not

I think of all the cleanup in Tohoku
the endless stretches of mangled homes
the tangled mountains of debris
and all the broken towns and families

that's where I should be, I think
that's where I'd be of more use
not here with Mom who doesn't need
me or Toby making her days harder
with our back talk

YiaYia is gentle
she's experienced
able to comfort her
better than us

but I hold my tongue
and don't say a word

on my bed Toby and I lean back against the headboard
and watch a Ghibli movie on Mom's computer

as the movie ends I try to discuss it in Japanese
but lately when I ask Toby something in Japanese
he answers in English like he's happy
to shed the language as if it were an extra coat

he seems to think it will be there for him
just hanging there
in the closet
waiting for him
whenever he wants to put it back on

later, before I go to sleep
in my journal I write a short poem

> lonely is when the language outside
> isn't the language inside
> and words are made of just 26 letters

and I wonder if
I should make it longer
then maybe one day
show it to Zena
or read it
at one of those workshops
at the Newall Center

Chapter 14

Breasts

the day before my next session
at the Newall Center
I text Sam on the cell phone
     that Toby and I are supposed to share
     but that I've claimed
asking if we can talk
maybe have pizza
after our writing sessions
before Chris picks us up

Sam replies *sure*

that day I also have dance club
and even though so much
is new to me
the captain Tracy
compliments me
on how fast I pick up
the moves
and on my style in the
catch steps
and height in the
fan kicks

and then the other girls
and the two guys in the club
start to talk to me
a little more

and the whole rest of the day
seems easier

on Wednesday
in my bag for the Newall Center
I put poems printed from websites
and copied from anthologies that
the school librarian helped me find—
one by Billy Collins
about tying a poem to a chair
to beat the meaning out of it
another by Li-Young Lee about his father
watching his mother put up her hair
and one by Lucille Clifton about hips
which is the one I decide to start with
because I think it will make Zena smile
especially that last line

and it does
her mouth goes wide
she does that throaty growl
and spells *a-g-a-i-n*

after I read the hip poem again
I read Li-Young Lee's
about putting up hair
then I ask Zena what we should
write about today

and she spells
b-r-e-a-s-t-s

I hold my breath
try to keep from blurting

in Japanese I'm good at controlling my words
but in English it's like I leave the gate open
and words dart out before I can catch them

so this time I close the gate on
the *no, anything but breasts*
that I want to say

then after a pause
a few breaths
I say *well, okay*
as long as we don't take turns
as long as she goes first

for a while I just say the colors of the letter board
     watch her eyes
     write the letters
     guess the words

the poem grows
and it seems Zena
has been thinking
about breasts all week
ever since I told her why
we moved here

Zena spells

14 Ways of Looking at a Breast

baby sanctuary
young girl's embarrassment
sexy woman's blessing
melon, nectarine, boob, bazoonga
permanent protuberance
excuse for lingerie
cause for coverage
bull's-eye
nourishment
comfort
source of pride
source of cancer
gravity's friend
half of a pair

but like eyes
even one
is better
than none

when she reaches the end
Zena looks exhausted, resting
then she glances at the letter board
and spells *u*

me? I say
she looks up

on breasts?
she looks up again

I'm not sure about this
I don't have any ideas
I tell her I'll think for a bit
scribble a while
then share

so I scribble
start to write

> *we never asked for them*
> *they just appear*
> *like bamboo shoots*

and I stop, realizing that Zena
coming from Massachusetts
probably doesn't know
how bamboo shoots push up
through the ground
how some grow tall as trees in days

Madoka's aunt, the one that's missing
had a room in her house
that was closed up and never used
and once she went in and found vines
lining walls and a bamboo shoot
poking up through flooring
already thigh high

but Zena is waiting
so I mess with my words
and at the top of my paper
draw a furry bamboo shoot
                           just coming up
through leafy soil

I show her the drawing of the shoot
and the hoelike tool for harvesting
and read my poem:

Breasts

we never asked for them
they just sprout like bamboo shoots
then someone comes along
with a tool
to harvest them

I glance at Zena
and my eyes tear
and I apologize
for writing such
a depressing poem

Zena looks up
then at the letter board
and she spells
i-t w-i-l-l b o-k
s-u-r-g-e-o-n-s h-a-v-e b-e-t-t-e-r t-o-o-l-s
t-h-a-n t-h-a-t

and I smile a little
and nod

I see it's nearly five
so I tell Zena I have to go
even though this isn't a very
cheery way to end our session
Zena doesn't look up

I raise the letter board
and Zena spells
s-o-o-n n-e-w c-o-m-p-u-t-e-r

new computer? for you?
how? I say *where'd the funding come from?*

p-r-i-v-a-t-e d-o-n-a-t-i-o-n-s she spells

wow! I say
your angels!

Zena spells
w-r-i-t-e m-o-r . . .

more poems?
she looks up
and I tell her
okay, you, too
and I turn to leave

but as I step out
a woman is coming in
oh, you must be the new poet!

I'm Emma I say

nice to meet you, Emma
I'm Anne, Zena's sister
usually here on Thursdays or Sundays
but this week is complicated

and Anne looks younger
all gesture and movement
like Zena is supposed to be
and suddenly I'm acutely aware
of all that Zena's lost
but then I'm glad for her
that she has this
      a visiting sister

Chapter 15

Pizza

when I find room 427
and pause at the doorway
Sam is still writing for Leap Sok

I listen at the threshold
to their lilting Khmer words
glance around the room
note the bright painting
of what I think is Angkor Wat

when I take a step forward
inside the room
Chea Pen squints at me
not quite seeing, it seems
Leap Sok stops talking
feebly waves me in
with what I realize is his only arm
I apologize for interrupting
and without thinking
greet them both by bowing
respectful Japanese-style

they all three look at me
amused

Sam says some words in Khmer, then says
you were born in Japan?

and I say *no, but lived there*
since I was a baby
Chea Pen and Leap Sok look to Sam
Sam says something to them in Khmer
and they both start to speak

Sam says
they want to know why—
are you a diplomat's kid?
army kid?

no, my dad works for a Japanese company I say
my mom teaches at a university
they met in Japan when they were college students
studying the language

Sam translates
there's some back-and-forth
then Sam says
they want to know about now—
the earthquake, the tsunami
did you come back because of radiation?
I already told them about your mother

and I'm surprised to know Sam knows about my mother
but then I remember he sat in YiaYia's living room
and he probably learned all sorts of things
from her
about us
about me

I say *no, we didn't come because of radiation*
our town is far from the damaged reactor
if my mother wasn't sick we'd be there
and I add
Japan's my home

I tell them that our furniture, our things
are still there in the house
my cat is still there with my friend
our home is still there
just not us

we'll go back I say
when my mother is better

Sam glances down
nods

then Sam gathers his things
sets the chair against the wall
has some conversation in Khmer
and places his hands together raising them
with a slight bow, muttering something
and adding in English
see you next week

what's that? I say in the hall
when you put your hands together

this? he says
      and raises his hands
      palms touching
      like he did in the room

sompeas he says
it's like a sign of respect—
when you greet a Cambodian
you do that and say
chum reap sour

I do *sompeas*
mumble the words
try to commit them to memory
for next week

outside it has started to rain
and feels cold enough to snow
even though it's only October

I wrap my scarf around my neck
and we hurry across the bridge against the wind
and into the heat of the pizza place

where we order slices
and I choose spinach
which at home I eat as *ohitashi*—
a side dish with ground sesame and soy sauce
but which I've never before eaten
on pizza

at the table we sit across from each other
with our slices and sodas
and I realize I've never done this
sit with a guy I hardly know
at a restaurant
without other friends around
and I'm suddenly nervous

to fill the silence I name pizza combos in Japan
     corn and tuna
     potato mayo
     teriyaki chicken
I tell him I like this spinach kind
that I can't get in Japan

but I feel idiotic sitting there with Sam
babbling on, *talking blather*
as Mr. Hays used to say in English class

I take a breath to slow myself
then we talk about poems and Zena
and Sam says there was another poet
who worked with her for a couple years
a guy who graduated last year and is now
at college and that's why they wanted me
to work with Zena

but I'm not a poet I say
I just write stuff in my journal
or for school

whatever Sam says
if you work with Zena
you'll be writing tons of poems—
that guy who worked with her and
who I bet is her "sexy man"
started writing and ended up winning a contest
and got a scholarship to a university
where they have a special creative writing program

I ask Sam what he did with Leap Sok today
and he says mostly Lok Ta Leap
was correcting his mistakes in Khmer

he says his mother has always made him study Khmer
but it's not as good as his English
our high school doesn't offer Khmer, you know
that's why my mother and stepfather
wanted me to stay in Lowell
where the high school has it
at all different levels

I'm confused—I say
your mother?
I thought you lived with your uncle

I do, but I have a mother . . .

and a stepfather? I ask

and a stepfather he says
plus a father—
loads of adults
want one?

no thanks I say
I'm good for adults
and we laugh

I ask why he lives with Chris
and not his mother
or father

he says
it's complicated
and I think, okay
note to self:
        don't ask about family

I finish the part with the cheese and spinach
and I'm chewing my way through thick crust
when he says
my mom's Khmer
she was supposed to marry a Khmer
but she worked and went to community college
then started classes at the university
where she met my father, Chris's brother
then got pregnant

I nod, set down my crust
wait for him to continue

after they got married
things were okay for a while
my dad finished school
got a job in New Hampshire
and they moved
but she hated it there
so they fought
and he started drinking
and she moved back to Lowell
and I went back and forth
between New Hampshire and Massachusetts
then after the divorce she married a Cambodian dude
and had two more kids

whoa I say
when he pauses to
start in on his second slice
so how old are they?

Van, my little brother, is seven
my sister Lena's ten

there's more he says

Sam continues
my dad was kind of a mess
so I came back to Lowell
moved in with my mom and stepfather
but their apartment's ultra-small
and I had to sleep in the living room
because Lena and Van had the other bedroom
so I stayed out a lot
messed up in school, drank a lot
made my stepfather mad
and my mother didn't know what to do
and it all just made me and them crazy
so finally I ran away
stayed with the older brother of a friend
and eventually I called Chris
and he came and got me

that was three years ago

it was supposed to be just temporary he says
but after a while everyone just
agreed to let me live there
with Chris and Beth

it's better he adds
and looks down

I don't drink at their house
never have
so it's not a temptation

I sit motionless
thinking through all he just said

Sam finishes his second slice
and picks up our paper plates

do you see your mom a lot? and stepfather? I ask

most weekends he says
as he stands and tosses our plates
into the trash

your father?

hardly ever he says
it's not good for me to be around him
I go to AA
but he still drinks

then I'm not sure
if I should
but I ask
*did your Mom live in Cambodia
during Pol Pot?*

and he sits down again and says
*when the Khmer Rouge took power
she was four
her father and oldest brother
were killed the first year
then a little sister and a brother died—
from sickness, malnutrition
and her mother was taken away . . .
then my mom and her older sister and brother
were separated
but found each other
and finally made it to a border camp*

*they got out in '81
when she was ten*

I think of the film
of Dith Pran laboring in the mud
starving so much he ate lizards
nearly killed again and again
finally making his way to the Thai border

she must be incredibly strong to have survived I whisper
and lucky

but he says
strong, weak
lucky, unlucky
who knows
and looks away

then we hear a honk
and through the window see
Chris has pulled into the parking lot
so we pick up our bags
and step outside into the cold

but Chris gets out of the car
walks around to the passenger side
and Sam climbs into the driver's side

what . . . ? I say
as I climb in

I'm driving Sam says

I stare at him

why not? I'm seventeen
and in a week I'll have had
my license six months
then I can drive friends
without this guy tagging along
and Sam pokes Chris in the arm

I suck in my breath
buckle my seat belt
Sam backs out slowly
pulls onto the main road
and starts to drive
with Chris giving advice
every other second
for which I'm grateful
because it seems too weird
to be in a car driven by someone
practically my age
in the dark
in rain
that makes the road
hard to see

in Japan
you can't get your license
till you're eighteen
I say

good rule! Chris says

how old are you?
Sam asks in the rearview mirror
when we stop at a light
sixteen?

in January I say

then at the next light he says
so . . . you get your permit in January
take driver's ed in the spring
and get your license in July

I nod at his eyes in the mirror
if I'm still here I say

they drop me off at YiaYia's
and Sam says
see you next week
or maybe before

and my stomach turns one way
hoping for before
and wishing next week
were tomorrow

but then my stomach turns another way
because in one week
there'll be just one week more
to my mother's surgery

Chapter 16

Hey

I actually see Sam
in the hall the next day
pass him when he's talking
with a group of guys built like him
not so tall but lean, broad-shouldered and muscled
one of them, Jae-Sun, I know from Model UN
and another, Tim, from biology

Sam looks up when I pass
and I say *hey*
and he says *hey* back
and from the sound of it after I pass
he's getting teased

this week in Model UN
we're working on writing resolutions
and practice position papers for our countries

Jae-Sun tells me I'll probably make the team
to go to the Boston conference at the end of January
and maybe even New York in May

I don't say anything about how I hope
we're not living here at the end of January
            and certainly not by May
how I hope we're back in Japan by then

in dance club Tracy
and choreographer Claire
teach us more moves for the jazz routine
we'll do during basketball halftimes
and it's harder than I expected
fast and full of leaps and fan kicks
pirouettes and fouettés
I haven't done in a while

so later, at YiaYia's
I roll up the rug in our bedroom and practice—
      dark outside, curtains open
      the bedroom window
      as my mirror

on Saturday
I start a new position paper
do grocery shopping with YiaYia
work on homework
practice dance moves
start another letter
download new music
do more Model UN

but I'm bored
tired of Venezuela
tired of this neighborhood that's not near anything
where you have to have a car
even just to get a bottle of shampoo

so I text Sam
and wait

I don't hear from him
till it's practically dark
when he texts
poetry workshop at Newall
where were u?
2morrow dance practice
now at my mom's in Lowell

and I text
hey! no one told me about a workshop!
I would have been there!!!

and he texts
sorry! next time
and in fact it's fine by me that I missed
since I'm really just learning
how to help Zena
but still, I hope Lin
or her sister, Anne
or someone
was there for her

then I'm thinking
dance?
he wrote *dance?*

and all weekend I'm wondering
what kind
        hip-hop? jazz? ballroom? ballet?

and why isn't he at school dance club meetings
with those other two guys?

all weekend long
I'm thinking
hey

Chapter 17

Noodles

Sunday morning Mom, Toby and I
go with YiaYia
to her Greek church

as we drive into Lowell
past huge homes that YiaYia says
once belonged to mill owners
across a bridge into the center of town
with old factory buildings and apartment blocks
I'm wondering where Sam's mother lives
or if I might catch a glimpse of Sam
on the street

YiaYia's church is huge
with gold domes topped with crosses
modeled after churches in Constantinople she says
which is Istanbul I want to say

inside are long windows of stained glass
a curved wooden balcony
saints painted on the ceiling
even puffy clouds

I don't mind being there
since I've never had the chance
to be in a building like this
just staring up
watching the light
beam down

at the coffee social afterward
we're introduced to the priest
and all of YiaYia's friends
and two breast cancer survivors

even Mom is smiling, relaxed
not pinched and overrevved
like she often is these days
as if she's psyching herself up
for a marathon

after we leave the church
we drive slowly through a downtown
of shops and restaurants
where I'd like to get out and walk around
but YiaYia's at the wheel and she says
she has sandwich makings at home

we pass signs for sushi
spring rolls
and pad thai
and my mouth waters
for rice
noodles
bean sprouts
seaweed
anything
but the pasty taste
of egg salad
or chicken salad
or tuna fish sandwiches

on Monday I see Sam once
as I'm making my way into the cafeteria
but he doesn't see me
and we don't even get to say *hey*

after school I hang out in the library
going through the poetry collection
searching for poems for Zena
and while I'm reading one of the   oems

at first I think it's just the irregular line breaks
the space the poet made   tween words
but I look up
at the sh lves
at t   librarian
and the spot fo lows

        grows

I pack my bag
call YiaYia
tell her to come get me

then I go outside the school
sit on a low stone wall
my head in my hands
eyes closed
waiting

but YiaYia doesn't arrive
and she still
only uses her cell phone
to make, not receive, calls

I set my pack in my lap
fold my arms
put my head down
try to stay calm

but I'm already half blind
and soon I'm shivering

inside the school
I make my way
along the wall
to the nurse's office
and drop onto a bed

then sit up
and throw up
into a wastebasket

by the time I wake
to the sound of Mom's voice
speaking to the nurse
the crescent of triangles has left
but numbness claims one arm
plus my tongue and jaw
and my head pounds and stabs

I lean on her
my eyes closed
as we walk out
the quiet school
to the car

then I fall across the backseat

she says something to me as she drives
I catch

                YiaYia mistake
Newall

                                    forgot
    high school
                        drive

but I can't piece anything together
can't make sense
or speak

and at YiaYia's
she puts me to bed

later I wake in the bed
set up in the study
for my mother's recovery
            hungry

the house is dark and still
and in the kitchen
lit by streetlight
I make myself a piece of toast

I dip a spoon into the
jar of *yuzu* preserves
eat a whole mouthful of the sweet-sour
then take another heaping spoonful
and spread it on the toast

after the toast I open the pantry
and find the instant miso ramen
Dad brought us and I heat some water
without letting the kettle whistle

when the ramen is ready
I hoist myself up to sit
on the kitchen counter
and slurp my noodles
by bluish ghostly streetlight

maybe in the future
I hear Shin say

don't change
I hear Madoka say

even you, Emma-chan
I hear her grandmother say

hey I hear Sam say

and I think
I don't know my life anymore

Chapter 18

Running

I sleep late the next day
and Mom drives me to school in YiaYia's car
I don't say anything and neither does she
until we're nearly at the school driveway

I think you should start running she says

hmm I say

I hate running

I like sports
I play sports
I'm good at sports
and dance
but I hate
just
running

if I were in Japan
I'd be playing volleyball
maybe on varsity
practicing for the tournament
and taking Saturday classes
at the dance studio . . .

here Toby has middle school soccer
but for me there's just dance club

I swallow my thoughts
hold my tongue

maybe I say to my mother
just before I get out of the car

but it doesn't end there
when I get home from school
she insists on taking me for a run

she plays the guilt card
so I can't refuse:
> *I'll show you a loop*
> *you can do on your own*
> *even when I can't*

Mom's fast
     she does 5 to 10 kilometers
     most every day
     and runs in charity races
     several times a year
     she's a dedicated runner
     with a lean runner's body

I'm out of shape now
not sinewy like her

but my legs are longer
so after a while
we find a pace
that suits us both

it's a thirty-minute run
that seems to go on and on

down long streets
   into a neighborhood
      of houses with lawns
         big as family farms in Japan
            and on those lawns more play equipment
               than any playground in the city of Kamakura
         and next to the houses
      garages for two or three cars
   and porches and gardens
   and huge shade trees
      dropping their leaves
      as we run past

I'm short of breath at first
but get into the rhythm
and the autumn air
and our breathing at last

until we come to a road
where three leaf blowers
blare at once

I sprint
to get by them
sprint
the final leg
but Mom pumps

                        past

in a blur
and beats me
to YiaYia's stairs

Chapter 19

L-a-t-e

on Wednesday
I have two tests, one in Chinese
        easy 'cause of Japanese
another in biology
        on prokaryotic reproduction
and a Model UN meeting at lunch
so it's not until I've closed my locker
at the end of the day that I realize
I forgot to prepare poems for Zena

in the library
I pull up a website and quick
print out a poem
I found last week

I arrive at the Newall Center late
having missed the bus I normally ride

and Zena is sitting up
in her repaired wheelchair
arms folded tight like birds' wings
legs hidden under a blanket
and her eyes are fierce
darting from me
to the letter board
back and forth

I pick it up
u r l-a— she spells

late, I know, I'm sorry
and I apologize for missing
the workshop on Saturday
but no one told me

I peel off my jacket
grab the poem I copied
and read aloud—Jane Kenyon's
"Otherwise" which I'd found
and shared with my mother
who hung it on the refrigerator
declaring
> *I like this Jane woman—*
> *good attitude!*
because my mom knows
that this Jane woman died of cancer

when I first read it on the computer
I liked the little everyday moments
the poet described and seemed to savor
so I now suggest to Zena that we do the same
> make an otherwise poem
> of simple moments that we savor

but Zena doesn't look up

finally Zena spells
d-i-d t-h-a-t

you did that already? I ask
and she looks up
what do you mean? I say
with the guy before me?
she looks up again

oh I say
sitting there stunned
the room feeling hotter and hotter
I take off my sweater, unwind my scarf

what should we do then? I say
and I swear she tries to drill holes
in my eyeballs with her glare

do you have a poem in your head? I ask
are you ready to write?
but Zena doesn't look up

so I think about other poems I read that week
even though my migraine
seems to have blasted my fragments
of poem memory apart

finally I recall one by Garrett Hongo
whose Japanese last name caught my eye
one that told a story of a man, killed
as he put his laundry in his car
so I tell Zena that I like how that poem
tells a story of an actual incident
then reflects on it
and maybe we can do that

Zena scowls
spells *n-o p-o-e-m?*

I bow, apologize

she spells *g-e-t i-t*

I try to argue
that we don't have much time
that I can remember some lines
that I can pull it up on my phone
that I can bring a copy next week
but her eyes are piercing cold
so I go to one of the nurses' stations
ask if they would do me a favor
      go to the poetry website and
      please please please
      print out a copy of that poem
      "The Legend"

they do and I go back to Zena
and read and show the poem to her

I read "The Legend" again and then I wing it
sharing my reaction about
the language the dying man spoke
that no one could understand
and explaining the weaver girl
mentioned at the end
and how she wants to meet the cowherd
on the other side of the heavenly river
which is part of Tanabata
the summer star festival
which we celebrate each year
by hanging paper wishes on bamboo

but still Zena glares

so I suggest thinking of incidents
we can write about and react to
ideas? I ask
she doesn't look up

I brainstorm out loud

> about a time I saw a man offer guidance
> to a blind man at a train station
> then walked him straight into a pillar

> about a time I found a photo album
> in tsunami sludge and Madoka's grandfather
> took me to return it to the owner
> who gave me a salted plum

> about a time I watched a man surfing
> with his dog

and finally Zena stops glaring
and her face twitches
into a smile

I tell her the dog had great balance
and barked for more

I suggest we each
think up incident poems
for the next time we meet

I don't say *next week*
because, with the surgery
I doubt that I'll
make it next week

she spells
d-o-n-t b l-a-t-e

I rush out and find Sam
as he's leaving room 427
you're late he says
Lok Ta Leap was asking
so I stick my head in
say hello with my hands together
in *sompeas* like Sam does
kind of like we do in Japan
      after tossing a coin into an offering box
      or before we eat a meal
but I can't remember the words
so I just smile
then we walk down the corridors
and out the doors into cold evening

what are the words again?
that greeting?

chum reap sour he says

and I say it over and over
    chum reap sour
    chum reap sour
    chum reap sour

and Sam looks at me
amused

I can give you a ride Sam says

he explains he has Chris's car
every Wednesday from now on
can take it to school
if he keeps up his grades

which isn't so easy for me he says
I'm okay discussing
but not writing or analyzing
or comparing and contrasting
I'm better with action
gymnastics
dance

like hip-hop and stuff? I say

yeah
and stuff he says

we walk to the street
where he's parked the car
and I get in the passenger side
and shut my door

and all at once
the space feels close

our breath fogging the windshield
seat belts sliding over jackets
Sam turning the key
in the ignition

he pulls onto the road
turns up the fan heater
maneuvers the car
through an intersection

Madoka would never believe this—
me in a car being driven
by a seventeen-year-old guy

I want to ask him to drive me anywhere
        except YiaYia's
but I don't think that would sound quite right

I tell Sam about the disaster
of a session I had with Zena
how I didn't think someone
who can only use her eyes
could make me feel so stupid

he tells me that some days are like that
Zena's not always sweet
the other guy walked out on her twice
eyes show a lot he adds
Cambodian dancers smile
with just their eyes

and I straighten, alert
that's the kind of dance you do?
Cambodian?

yeah—folk and classical
plus hip-hop

cool I say, not knowing exactly
what Cambodian dance is
but thinking of an Indonesian dancer
who performed at the art museum by the shrine
and Thai dancers at the international school last year
> their fingers extending back
> their hands fluid, dancing

Sam says
the dance troupe's great
it keeps me in line

then real quick
he changes topics
next week I can drive you to the Newall Center
just meet me in the school parking lot

and my face goes hot
as I say *thanks*
wondering
        does this mean more
            than just a ride?

then I remember

actually I can't go next week—
my mom's surgery

oh, right he says

and I want him to say more
or stop the car so we can talk
without jumping topic to topic
without me blathering
because just thinking of that day
and what they'll do to her
makes me breathe too fast

but Sam's quiet
headlights and streetlights flash past
and soon we're at the intersection
where we turn into YiaYia's neighborhood
and when he slows in front of the house
YiaYia's already peering out the window

I say *thanks* and step out
knowing I'll soon hear
for the third time this afternoon
you're late

Chapter 20

Camfood

Thursday afternoon at Model UN
my partner, Monica
says Jae-Sun told her
I like one of the gymnasts

gymnasts? I ask

she says *yeah*
that Vietnamese dude
the one who's really good—
like, one of the best on the team

oh I say *you mean Sam?*
he's Cambodian

oh, well, I was close
anyway, do you?

what? I say

like him? Monica says

and fortunately I don't have to answer
because just then we are meeting all together again
to go over position papers ·
and Jae-Sun is within earshot

that night after dinner I'm watching TV with Toby
when I get a text

it's Sam—

and I don't know if I'm just tired
from the longer run I did after school
adding an extra loop at the end
or stressing about the surgery or what
but Sam's words make me tear up

what? Toby asks
when he sees me wipe my eyes

he hits the remote
drops the volume
but I can't speak
what? he says

I show him the text
chris wants 2 no if you can come 2 din
sat night . . . your whole fam . . . camfood

but that's good Toby says

I nod

he punches me
baka! he says—jerk!
don't confuse me
I thought it was more bad news

I rub my arm
wipe my eyes
blow my nose

realizing from the punch
that underneath
Toby worries, too

I text Sam back
sounds good—camfood?

and he answers
cambodian food, dodo

and I laugh and show Toby
and we high-five 'cause
we are both so aching
for Asian food

not that I really know what Cambodian food is like
but I suspect it's similar to Thai or Vietnamese
which we love

in Kamakura there's a Vietnamese café
where Madoka, Shin, Kenji and I go
to have *pho* at tables outside
eating to the *kan kan kan* sound
of the train crossing

and thinking of that café
and my friends
I'm homesick
but I'm also thinking
of dinner with Sam

and how

      if someone offered me a ticket to Japan this minute
      maybe, just maybe, I wouldn't want to go back today
      because of what I'm looking forward to tomorrow

Mom and Toby are game for the dinner
but YiaYia suggests we go without her
I urge her to come
but I know for a fact
she doesn't like much Asian food
            except teriyaki
            which she pronounces *terry-ackee*

go without me
enjoy
she says
to be honest
I could use a quiet evening
and she winks at me

I call Sam to say thank you and yes
but Chris answers Sam's phone
Sam Nang's driving he says

uh-oh I joke
thinking it's strange
that Chris says Sam's last name

I tell Chris we can come to dinner
and ask what we can bring

nothing—
Sam Nang's mom, Lily
will be cooking
with everyone's help
just bring yourselves

Chapter 21

Sweet and Sour

the next night
is a great night
Sam's mother, Lily, has made
a sweet-and-sour lemongrass soup
that fills my lungs when we enter the kitchen
and while she prepares curried fish she calls *amok*
Sam, Beth, Sam's sister Lena and I
make spring rolls

Lily is kind
solid-looking and laughing
strong but funny with Lena and Van
not at all how I'd imagine for a survivor
if your father, sister and brother were killed
and your mother disappeared
when you were young
and you'd nearly starved
and became a refugee

we place shrimp on rice paper rounds
add noodles, greens and scallions
fold in one end and roll it all up

it's like the *gyoza* parties at Madoka's house
where we made dumplings, all kinds—
pork and scallion, cabbage and shrimp
tomato and cheese . . .

we talk as we fill the spring rolls
people come in and out of the kitchen
Mom takes Lena and Van to the dining room
to teach them Japanese handkerchief play
and I ask Lily if she was from the city
or the countryside in Cambodia

she tilts her head as she looks at me
says *countryside, first, then Phnom Penh*
I ask if she's been back and she says *once*
I took Sam Nang, about three years ago

I ask how it was
half to Sam, half to his mother
and his mother tilts her head again
and Sam tilts his head the same way

Sam says *different*
especially the village
where most of our relatives live

how so? I say

like simple, you know—
no running water, cows walking down the road
dusty, no electricity, lots of kids
lizards, palm trees
hot

then Lily asks me to tell her about
our town in Japan

I say it has lots of temples
that there's a temple at the end of our lane
and temple bells gong at six a.m. and six p.m.
I tell her it's an old city
with ancient harbor stones off the beach
and hiking trails in the hills
and hidden cave tombs
and again I'm babbling
but I'm guessing
she must know what it's like
to miss a place
so different from where you are

she asks about the tsunami
and I tell them about Madoka's family
the aunt still missing
and how I wish I could be there helping

then I ask if Lily dances, too
the folk, the classical
no, I only tried it in the camps she says

refugee camps? I ask
Lily nods
some dancers who'd survived
taught us

Lily turns back to the stove then
which I think means
I shouldn't ask more
so I ask Sam what he'll be dancing
in the upcoming performance

some folk and I think one classical he says

get him to show you the DVDs
Beth says as she walks by
the one from the water festival
and the one from the state college

so after we finish making spring rolls
Sam takes me into Chris's art studio
and we sit down in front of a beat-up desk
surrounded by Chris's sketches tacked to the walls
and paintings leaning and stacked everywhere

Sam slides a DVD into a computer
and fast-forwards
and there he is onstage
dancing with some basket things

this is the fishing dance
those are fish traps he says
and suddenly I'm in another world

Toby comes in, leans over us, says
hey! like soran
which is exactly what I'm thinking—
soran bushi and other folk dances we learned
for school sports festivals in Kamakura
and that I later danced with a *yosakoi* team

Sam skips forward on the DVD
and then he's a monkey with a mask
one of several onstage scratching, leaping
somersaulting, playing with his tail
doing cartwheels and back handsprings

and he's lithe and athletic and amazing

then he skips again and says
here's a classical dance—
not me, but maybe soon . . .
I want that part—Hanuman

and he points to a character in white
with a dagger and monkey mask
dancing opposite a girl
with an ornate gold tail
it's from the Reamker he says
the Cambodian Ramayana

oh I say
and think
note to self:
      learn about the Reamker

and Sam says
this is the part where Hanuman the monkey king
finds the mermaid who's stealing the stones
for making the bridge to the island
where Sita is being held

and I look at Sam
who's staring intently at the screen
and maybe, the girl

and I am suddenly filled with
envy and awe
and other feelings
that make my face go warm

then Beth comes in with Mom and Lena
and she asks Sam to go back to the monkey dance
and we watch that dance again to the end
then the music changes from classical Cambodian
to hip-hop and the monkeys break into crazy moves
and Van is jumping around mimicking them

when they all leave the room
I ask Sam to show me the fishing dance again
I tell him I learned some folk dances in Japan
and explain about my *yosakoi* team

how long have you been doing this? I ask

*since I moved back to Lowell
when I was twelve*

why didn't you tell me? I say
and it sounds accusing
which is not at all what I'd meant

but it seems like such a big part of him
and I don't know why but
I'm suddenly jealous . . .
the dance? the girl?
*I had no idea you dance
so seriously, I mean*

Sam says *well, it's hard to explain
Americans don't get this
unless they see it*

I bristle
Americans?
I'm American and I get it
and in Japan we dance folk dances
and Obon dances all the time
which is a stupid thing to say
because people hardly dance them
all the time

but I can't seem to stop my tongue

not all Americans are the same
and anyway, you're *American*

he skips the DVD back
to another classical piece
with five girls dancing
silver cups in hand

he turns from the computer to me
as the girls toss something from the cups
and waits until I look at him

hey he says

I swallow
glance at him
hey I say back

we return to the kitchen
and help his mother ready the feast
she speaks to him in Khmer
then switches to English
and back to Khmer
and suddenly I realize
from the way his mother speaks to him
from the way Chris and Beth speak to him
and from some forms and papers on the refrigerator
that say *Samnang Gill*
that "Sam" is Samnang
not Sam Nang

and I feel like a complete
and total
dodo

Samnang
Samnang
Samnang
I say to myself
and I wonder if I ever
actually called him Sam
to his face

Sam . . . Samnang offers me some juice
coconut or tamarind
I go for tamarind
and he pours from a can
into two glasses with ice
and gives me one

then in a corner of the kitchen
he lifts his glass to me and says softly
so the others don't hear
here's to different Americans

and I smile gratefully and
take a sip

and think
maybe, just maybe
he didn't realize I was calling him
Sam
all this time

Lena and Van's handkerchief skit
about a rabbit, goldfish and butterfly
who trick a noisy cicada
into being quiet

is followed by an amazing meal
set on mats spread on the living room rug
and Lily's pleased to see
that we're fine sitting on the mats
and that we love everything

Beth tells me it's great that I'm running
to help eliminate stress and asks if I experience
creative bursts during migraines
but I shake my head
not so far

Mom asks Chris about his painting and design work
the classes he teaches at an art school
Lily asks Toby to teach her some Japanese words
Samnang talks about his upcoming performance
Van is begging for more handkerchief tricks

and though I'm eating foods I've never eaten before
and though we're with a family in Massachusetts
we've never dined with before
this is the most I've felt at home
since we left Japan

then partway through dessert
Lily makes some reference
to Samnang's friend Say-something
asks about her twisted ankle
and how she's dancing

I keep my eyes on the coconut pudding
my spoon slicing through it
ask *how do you spell that?*
so I don't make any more name mistakes
and Lily says *S-e-r-e-y*
it means freedom

but in my peripheral vision
I catch Chris and Beth glancing at me
and at Sam . . . Samnang
and I can practically feel him
tensing on the mat beside me

Samnang says something to his mother
in Khmer
she answers him sharply
in Khmer
and he says something back
and I am no dummy
I notice
when Chris abruptly changes the subject
and talks over Lily when she tries to say
something further on the subject of Serey

later, when we leave
Samnang hangs back by his mother
and Beth walks beside me to the car
and whispers *sorry*
I'm not quite sure what that was all about

but nobody needs to tell me
what it's all about

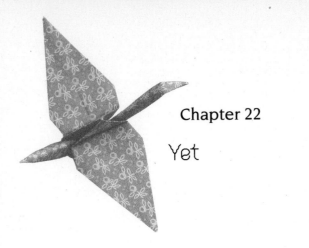

Chapter 22

Yet

Sunday I wake up way too early
in a way foul mood
and I wish things were as simple
as flicking switches
        some thoughts on
        some thoughts off

I find Samnang Gill on Facebook
but don't friend him yet

I go for an early-morning run
and do sit-ups
and push-ups
and other self-inflicted punishment
I decline YiaYia's offer to go to church
not really wanting to be near Lowell
just in case I see Sam . . . Samnang

I'm hoping Samnang will text
and say something like
   sorry about that Serey stuff
   she's just my cousin
or something else to deny
that he has a girlfriend

then just after I've showered and dressed
Toby flies into the room
with the computer open
and there is Madoka
waving at me

oh my God! I say

you forgot! she says *didn't you!*

behind her are Kenji, Shin and Kako
and they are all laughing
because my hair is not even combed
and I really did forget that we had
emailed and agreed on this time

it's so weird to see them there
in Madoka's living room
while I'm here in YiaYia's house
and we all start talking at once—
they're asking questions
I'm asking questions
and the words get Skype-garbled
slow down! I tell them

they ask about my school life
and how much I weigh
and then they all cover their ears
like I'm talking too loud

finally when I ask Madoka
about her grandparents and relatives
the others are quiet

Madoka says they're doing okay
that it's getting cold up there
that her grandparents will visit
Kamakura at New Year's

your aunt? I ask
not yet she says
meaning they still
haven't recovered
her body

then Madoka's mother appears
Emma-chan, how are you?
take good care of your mother!

then her mother leaves
Shin and Kenji say good-bye
Kako, too
it's already ten-thirty at night there
and they need to go home

then, when it's just Madoka and me, she says
you know . . .
when your mom finished talking with my mom
and your mom gave the computer to Toby
as Toby was walking upstairs with the computer
Shin asked Toby if you have a boyfriend yet
and Toby said . . . well, maybe

I groan
no!
what did Shin say?

he said yappari—of course
so? do you? Madoka asks

tell Shin it's not even a maybe I say

but Madoka's brows are raised
her eyes bore into mine

at least not yet I add

and then we're laughing
and I tell her all that's been going on
with school, and Zena, and dance club pirouettes
and fouettés and a little about Samnang

Madoka theorizes that Serey is Samnang's
stepsister or aunt or daughter
and we're yakking almost as fast
and crazy as if we were in the same room
and she's saying don't worry about Shin
because he's got his eye on some girl in the archery club
then Mom comes in to announce that my grandparents
have arrived from Vermont

and I have to tear myself away from Madoka
to step back into America

Chapter 23

American Treasures

Gram and Gramps
my mother's parents
hug us and hold our hands
and once I've combed my hair
they drive Toby, Mom, me and YiaYia
to Newburyport where we walk along
the waterfront and among the old houses

we're at the mouth of the river
the exact same one that flows through
Lowell and YiaYia's town
but here I can't stop gulping the air
because it smells of the sea

at the restaurant where we stop for lunch
Gram and Gramps, who've visited us in Japan
ask about Madoka
and our cat Shoga
and Toby's friends
and if I'm keeping up my Japanese
and what foods we miss most
and if I'd like to come visit them in
Vermont for part of the winter break

for once I don't waste my energy
thinking I might not be here then
I tell them *sure*
even though I don't like winter
and all the gear you have to wear
and I've only ever been to Vermont
in summer

we'll make skiers of you yet says Gramps
and Toby fist-pumps
and when he kicks me
I do a mini fist pump, too

Gramps presents Toby and me
with wooden boxes he made with hinged lids
all decorated with carvings of ferns
to hold your American treasures Gram says

they're beautiful I say, then joke
but everything here is so big

Gramps says *true*
but I'm sure you'll find some small treasures
mementos of your time here

I tell him that later
I'll pick up a shell or pebble
or something to remember
this day in Newburyport
for my first treasure

then YiaYia and Gram and Gramps
present my mother with the long necklace
made of all different size and color beads

each bead
from a friend
or relative

all mailed in little packages to Gram
strung together on a silk cord by YiaYia
to give Mom strength
and positive thoughts
during surgery

Mom is quiet and gives
YiaYia, Gram and Gramps long hugs
and the waitress goes teary
when she learns the significance
of the hugs
   the beads on the table
     and the illustrated key to each bead
       that Gramps created

finally the sting
of all that Serey talk is dulled
and I forget about Samnang
and stop thinking about Shin
and what Toby said to him
and whether Madoka's relatives
feel abandoned by us

because I know
this is what I needed
and Mom needed today—
family

Chapter 24

Fear and Hope

the day before the surgery
Dad arrives

Mom picks him up at Logan
and they are both there
waiting for me, then for Toby
to get home from school
and when we're finally all together
we do a big goofy group hug

then Toby goes off to play soccer
like it's the most normal day of the year

Mom and Dad and I
go for a walk as the sun sets
and Mom picks up leaves
crimson, russet and gold
and the cold settles down upon us
as I update Dad
on school
Model UN
and Zena
skipping right over
Samnang

neither of them mentions dinner at Chris and Beth's
though Mom has probably filled him in
and maybe mentioned to him
something about Samnang
about Samnang and me
and what she might have thought
        was

but actually
        is not

Dad brought ingredients
for *okonomiyaki*
so when we get back to the house
he and I chop cabbage and scallions
peel and devein shrimp
mix the batter and cook
the big pancakes in a skillet

after we've started eating
Mom shuts her eyes as she chews
and tells us she could swear
she was back in Japan

but then a neighbor's car alarm goes off
she opens her eyes, says *guess not!*

Toby says *wait—close your eyes again*
and he whispers for us to make Japan sounds

so we do—
train crossing gates
temple bells
ambulances
min-min cicadas
musical trash trucks
motorcycle gangs
whistling kites
five-o'clock chimes
train announcements
lost-elderly announcements . . .

all in a crazy messy sequence
that has us cracking up
and YiaYia shaking her head
until Toby decides to throw in
some farts and burps and
that's the end of that

after dinner we go out for ice cream cones
because that's what Mom wants—
peppermint stick with chocolate sprinkles
or *jimmies* as YiaYia and Dad call them

but when we get home
suddenly it's not fun anymore
it's time for going over all the details
of tomorrow
       Mom's bag for the hospital
       the forms
       the instructions for YiaYia

I go upstairs to the room I share with Toby
sit on the bed with a pillow and atlas for a desk
but instead of homework
I take out the notebook
I use with Zena
stare at a blank page
and finally write
the word I've been
avoiding

    fear

and I think of other times
I've felt it

and write

    floors and walls
    ceilings and lights moving
    when they shouldn't

I turn the page
and stare at the paper
and think
and write

    hope

then

    outside repaired homes
    Madoka's cousins roll a ball
    for a snowman

I think some more
and write

    a missing breast
    on a running woman
    is hardly noticed

I'm about to turn the page
when my phone buzzes
and there's a text
from Samnang

good luck to your mom tomorrow
will call after school to check
      with no apology or explanation
      about that girl Serey

and I suppose I'm glad at least
to have this much from him

I text back
39

Dad comes into the bedroom with Toby
and they sit down on the edge of my bed
and I put the phone
and notebook away

Dad holds us close
one on each side
kisses us in turn
tells us not to worry
we have a tough mother
and it's a tiny bit of abnormality
that they want to remove so it doesn't spread
and the prognosis is good, good, good
and we need to hold on to that word
good

Chapter 25

Sci-fi

the next morning we're up early
Mom is wearing her bead necklace
and clutching the amulet
from Madoka's mother
and she is smiling
and looking tough
like she's headed out
for a road race

in the kitchen I hug her
Toby hugs her
YiaYia hugs her
then Mom doesn't want any more of that, says
okay, let's get this over with

Toby and I go out in our slippers
our fleeces over our pajamas
and wave as Mom and Dad
drive away in the dark
till the car's rear lights
turn out of sight
and even a little after
Japan-style

then we go inside and start to wait
even though it's not really time
to wait

we eat breakfast
watch TV
make tea
Gram and Gramps arrive
bake oatmeal raisin bars
and time crawls

finally I go for a run
around the hour
surgery is beginning
my cell phone in a pocket

the first mile or so
I feel wooden
like I should give this up

I slow my pace
nearly walk
but then my body clicks in
and I pick up speed

breathing
stepping
steady
thinking of Zena's words—

> *but like eyes*
> *even one*
> *is better*
> *than none*

back at the house
I shower
get dressed
sit on the bed
and wait

I take out my notebook
picture Zena
in the Newall Center
every day
waiting

I write

> *a mermaid swims*
> *through seaweeds wondering where*
> *her legs went*

then I can't focus
so I stand
try pirouettes

later I open my notebook again
and write

> *barking dog*
> *rides the wave to shore*
> *then barks for more*

and

> *Samnang!*
> *so, who is this girl Serey and how long have*
> *you been seeing her and what do you share*
> *besides Khmer heritage and dance?!*

because I realize suddenly Serey is probably
that girl who was dancing opposite Hanuman

I close my journal
try kanji practice
    writing characters
    in columns of fifteen boxes
    column after column
    to fill a page
    then another . . .
until the phone rings

I drop the workbook
fly downstairs
and it's Dad
saying Mom's in recovery
all went well
with the surgery
and he'll call again
in an hour or two
after she's been transferred
from ICU to her room

I don't know what to do for the next hour
so I open my dresser drawers
refold clothes
arrange my earrings in pairs
then go downstairs for lunch
which is moussaka
that YiaYia has made from scratch
the cinnamon
the meat
the potatoes
the eggplant
the topping
just right

finally we get another call
and Dad says Mom's in her room
not quite herself but doing well
and she said she might even be up
for a visitor or two
late afternoon or early evening
after she sleeps

a visitor or two?
how can you remove
a significant part of a person's body
and they can be talking
      talking!
about having a visitor or two?

I think
      there is something fundamental
      I don't understand about surgery

but suddenly I can breathe again
stop hunching my shoulders
and gritting my teeth

and I can't help it
even though I know he's in class
and won't get the message till later
I take out my phone to text Samnang
and tell him
all good, surgery done

and I email Madoka
and tell her the surgery went smoothly
okagesamade—thankfully

Chapter 26

Yes Yes Yes

Samnang calls as soon as classes are done

hey he says

but now I know
not to read too much
into that *hey*

hi I say

I share what we heard from Dad
and Samnang asks how I'm doing
much better I say

so, what do you think he says
you want to go see Zena?
I can pick you up on my way

and though I hadn't planned on it
and I haven't prepared poems
when he says this I realize
I'd love to see Zena today

I tell him okay if I can get home
in time to go to the hospital
in Boston with Gram and Gramps

they could meet us at that gas station
near the highway ramp he says
the one with the donuts—
we could get you there by 5:15

and in the back of my mind
I'm wondering why
he's being quite this nice to me
if he has a girlfriend

YiaYia, Gram and Gramps
are all opposed to the idea
of me going anywhere
and of Samnang driving me
but I think that's not fair

we call Dad
who consults groggy Mom

then Dad's back on the phone saying fine
telling me to thank Samnang for his trouble
and warning me to make sure he drives carefully

and I'm glad I never shared
about Samnang's drinking past—
          this is enough
          of the third degree

about half an hour later
Samnang pulls up
but when I go out to his car
I see there's another person inside
up front
          a girl

hi I say as I get in the back
and Samnang introduces me
          to Serey

*Serey's going to help two women
at the Newall Center today
while I work with Lok Ta Leap*

I nod
stunned to be in the car
with the two of them

Serey turns to me
Samnang told me about your mom
I'm sorry—I hope she recovers fast

I gulp some air
and say *thanks*
her presence
having taken me aback

and suddenly I'm so not wanting to be in that car
having so wanted a few minutes
alone with Samnang
even if he is
taken

then I ask
are you the dancer in that video
opposite Hanuman?
are you the mermaid?

you saw that? she says, surprised

and I say *yeah, Samnang showed me*
and I can see what seems like a flash of startle
as she glances at Samnang

I add quickly
you're an amazing dancer
when did you start?

when I was five she says
and for the rest of the ride I keep her talking
about how at first she liked dancing
just for the friends and performances
but now she's really committed to the troupe
and learning new dances, both folk and classical
especially after visiting Cambodia two years ago
and dancing for relatives who'd never seen the royal dancing
and after studying with master teachers who come to Lowell
from the Royal University of Fine Arts in Phnom Penh

I'm actually glad to be hearing Serey's words
not just because it's a relief
to know this girl of Samnang's is interesting
but also because I'm too fragile
to say anything about myself today

maybe it wasn't a good idea
to come after all
I want to curl up
take a nap
and I half wish
for a migraine

but when the car stops
I unbuckle, get out
and follow them inside
the Newall Center

where
as we go our separate ways
Serey seems to know her way around

when I get to room 448
Zena is in her chair
and she does this funny thing
looking up again and again and again
like *hooray! hooray! hooray!*
when I tell her the surgery was successful
and they didn't find anything unusual

of course I say
there's still the pathology report
and they took samples from the other breast
so we'll have to see about that
        which is something I haven't told anyone else

I ask Zena if she has an incident poem
and she looks up
but then she points with her eyes
not at the letter board
but at what I realize is a screen
attached to her chair
and I move around so I can see it
and gasp to realize it's a computer

with eye tracking? oh my God!
have you used it?

a l-i-t-t-l-e she spells slowly
moving her eyes
blinking to select letters
on the screen
l-e-a-r-n-i-n-g

cool! I say *but be patient, okay?*
new computers can be a pain
and I'm sure this is way more complicated

Zena looks up

then Zena spells that she's *t-i-r-e-d*
and indicates she wants to use the letter board
so I follow the rows of colors
and write down her poem
picking up on the pattern
saving her having to spell
the same phrases over and over

Zena spells:

My Sister

my sister said isn't she still in there?
the doctor said no
my sister said isn't it possible her brain is fine?
the doctor said no
my sister said I think she's crying
the doctor said no
my sister said I think she's angry
the doctor said no
my sister said Zena's in there, I know it
the doctor said no
but the OT said well, maybe she is
the OT said Zena, you look up when you mean yes, okay?
my sister said Zena, are you in there?
and I looked up and told her
yes

I read it aloud all the way through
look up OT on my cell phone
and skimming again
I feel my throat catch

Zena, is this true? I whisper
Zena looks up

I say
what a sister
and that OT . . .
man, they were definitely your angels!
and Zena looks up

I read it aloud again
and tell her I'll type it up
for her

then I take out the two poems I found online
just before Samnang picked me up

one, by a Kaylin Haught
which now seems even more appropriate
about God saying yes
to this girl about things like
wearing nail polish
and being short
all in this hilarious voice
that Zena loves

and another poem
that I read aloud twice
about a person painting a room
before leaving one country
to start a new life in another country

in the poem
there's a window
that seems to represent promise
        or possibility
and I tell Zena I like that part the best
and I thought we could write poems about
what we'd like to see through a window

I do what Mr. Hays used to do
when he gave us writing prompts
and suggest we just think
for a few minutes
and while we do
I stare out her window
        to a band of sky
        above tops of bare trees
        behind renovated mills

and think
of what I'd like to see out that window—
        the silhouette of Mount Fuji
        as the sun slides into it
        like a coin into a bank
        the way we'd see it from the
        seawall at the marina
        while *Yuyake koyake* chimes
        on the loudspeakers
        tell kids it's time to go home

then I'm thinking of what I'd like to see
from Madoka's grandparents' windows
            trees with new green
            garden walls repaired
            piles of debris
                    gone

and my thoughts jump around
from Kamakura
to Tohoku
to my mother
to Samnang
and Serey . . .

then I ask Zena if she's ready and she looks up
so I start listing the colors and letters
and she begins to spell her poem idea

Zena spells:

What I See

the window
frames a view:
young woman
with husband
two small children

flanking them
an older man and woman
proud grandparents
all posing for a photograph

she stops

I say
is that the end?
and she looks up

I'm reading it over again
then notice she's staring at the letter board
so I put my finger to it and say the colors

she spells *y-o-u-n-g w-o-m-a-n i-s u*

me? I say

and then I get it—
       the future
       the far future
       with my mother in it

and I nod and smile
well, then who's my husband?

s-e-c-r-e-t
Zena spells
and growls with her
mouth wide

we don't have time for my poem
because Samnang appears at the door ·
minus Serey, I note
and I apologize to Zena, saying
I have to go visit my mother
and Zena does that thing with her eyes
going up again and again and again
yes yes yes in affirmation
just like at the end of that poem
about the girl talking to God

so I bend down and kiss her
  right on the temple
  near her purple barrette
which startles both me
and her

see you next week I say

Chapter 27

Tubes

outside I ask Samnang about Serey
and Samnang says he'll come back for her
after he takes me to meet my grandparents

and I apologize for troubling him
but he says it's no problem
he's glad to help
and likes driving Chris's car

I ask him about Leap Sok
what they did today
and he says that Lok Ta Leap
was talking about before Pol Pot
when he lived in Battambang
after he left the temple where he was a monk

he was writing about climbing up
to these ruins at Wat Banan—
    this temple with a long stairway of stone steps
he was trying to describe the view from the top

what kind of view? I ask

360 degrees
rice fields, sugar palms
villages, a river

nice I say

yeah he says *makes me want to go there*

Samnang asks about my mother
when she'll be able to come home
and he's just as nice as always
and I'm completely confused and wonder

      did something change?

or did nothing change
and I was just a fool to think
he was somewhat interested in me before?

he doesn't say a word
to explain Serey
and I don't ask

Gram and Gramps are already waiting
at the gas station where we agreed to meet
Gram waves me over and hands me
oatmeal raisin bars for Samnang
which I hand him through his window
wanting to linger but wanting to go
then I nod-bow and he drives away

I climb into the backseat with Toby
and then we're off to the hospital
where we park in an underground garage
take an elevator up and enter the corridors

and I try not to look left
or right or even, sometimes
straight in front of me
to avoid seeing needles
and tubes and fluids

we find Mom's room
and she's actually sitting up
and smiling for God's sake
and we all go over to her
and kiss her in turn
and she's asking me about Zena and Samnang
and wants one of Gram's oatmeal bars
and I can't believe a body can do this—

       lose a part and act like
       it's nothing

I guess the surgeons do have
good tools

presurgery
Mom opted not to do
reconstructive surgery
> *I'm built small* she'd said
> *I'm a runner*
> *it won't take much of a falsie*
> *to match my other*

and now I'm glad she decided
on fewer procedures—
the simpler the recovery
the better

I say *aren't you in pain?*
and she says
some
but I'm on strong drugs
and slept a lot

and I'm so glad to see her cheerful
and to see the relief in her face
but as I'm standing there staring
        at her
        and the IV drip
        that attaches to her hand
        that pours stuff into her hand
        and a tube running into her pajama top

I try to gaze hard at just her eyes
but they start going dark
and she sees me looking
then I hear her
from far away
saying

                    Emma?

when I come to
I'm lying on the floor
and my father is leaning over me

Toby's on the floor beside Dad
pressing an ice pack to his forehead
and a nurse is telling me to
         lie still
as she adjusts a rolled-up towel
under my head

because apparently I fainted
and knocked over Toby
who whacked his head on the wall
and then I struggled and thrashed
and hit my dad, too

Toby's whining
jeez, Emma!

the nurse is saying
keep the ice pack on

Dad is rubbing his jaw
where I smacked him

Mom is saying
I'm so sorry, honey!

and Gram is saying
well, I was right on this one—
this visit was not
a good idea

Chapter 28

Costume

Mom comes home the next day
and is there propped up with pillows
on the bed in YiaYia's study
when I get back from school

she's not cheerful
she's hurting
and I'm careful to be quiet
when I'm with her

I help Dad with the stuff I can do—
     get her water
     take her snacks
     adjust her pillows

but I stay far away
when the visiting nurse comes
and they're dealing with
         the dressings
         and that drain thing

I go out for a run
hoping that if I run each day
sleep eight hours each night
eat on a regular schedule
I can fend off the migraine
that's just waiting to sock me
after all this stress

as I run, my mind wanders
          stuff I recall
          stuff I have to do
and about halfway through the run
I suddenly remember
Halloween is Monday
which is
          before
my next visit with Zena
and I promised I'd help
with her costume

so all through the second half of my run
I'm wondering how on earth
I can create a mermaid costume
that will fit on someone
who can't move

back at the house I ask YiaYia
who loves crafting
and right away has ideas
so after I shower
we leave Dad with Mom
and go to a mall

we buy a camisole with built-in bra
then at a fabric store pick up
odds and ends from sale bins
and a couple yards
of shiny purple satin

on Friday after school
we plan it out
and on Saturday
we get to work
for real

YiaYia's amazing
she sits with me, guides me
at her sewing table
which used to be in the den
but is now upstairs squeezed
into her bedroom

we cut the back of the camisole off
refinish the sides
sew shell shapes
over the boobs
then use our newspaper pattern
to fashion a mermaid body
and tail in purple

I try it on YiaYia
who holds her arms folded tight like wings
and keeps her legs immobile as she sits on a chair
I place the camisole top over her front
then drape the purple bottom over her lap
Velcro it to the tank
and arrange the tail
to cover her feet

when Mom wakes up
we seat YiaYia in the chair
beside Mom's bed in the study
and show Mom what we've made

nice! she says
but you need something
for her hair

YiaYia and I look at each other
go back upstairs to the sewing machine
and create a shell of shiny purple fabric
to glue onto a barrette

Saturday night I Skype-call Madoka
from Mom's computer in my bedroom
and Madoka's voice is as clear
as if I'm two doors away

I tell her about Mom's surgery
and ask if she can video-Skype
but she says she can't now because of
extra band sessions and practice
for her private sax lessons
but she'll figure out a good time soon

I tell Madoka about fainting in the hospital
and Zena and the mermaid costume
and I'm laughing and it feels so good
to speak Japanese again
even rushed and brief like this

but then Madoka interrupts

they found the body she says

what? your aunt?

on Monday
diggers found her
they identified her
by her dental records

and then the air leaves me
and I can't speak and I'm gasping
and I squeak out *why didn't you say?*

well, your mother's surgery
anyway, there's a service next weekend
we'll be going up

I fumble for the right words in Japanese—
how it's such a difficult thing
how I'm glad they can say a proper farewell
then I add *light some incense for me, okay?*

I have to go she says
I whisper *take care*

I clap a hand to my mouth
and it's Toby who finds me crying
and I tell him this time
it's good news
and bad

and together
we tell our mother and father
and my grandmother

and that night we light a candle
and set it on the table
in YiaYia's kitchen
and bow our heads
to remember

I try to focus on Zena
and the costume
try to keep from thinking
of the little cousins
and their seven months missing
mother now found

and finally I call Samnang
to ask if he's free on Sunday
to take me to see Zena
to give her the costume

but just as I ask him
I recall he has dance
never mind I start to say
but he says *sure*
if we go around noon
I'll see if I can get the car

and I'm so relieved
for his kindness again
and then I can't help it
hope flickers inside me

but then he adds
I'll ask Serey if she wants to come, too
we can take Lok Ta Leap
and Lok Ta Chea some sweets

and I say to myself
       WHAT was I thinking?

Chapter 29

Mermaid

Sunday we go early
to YiaYia's church
and say prayers
and light a candle for
Madoka's aunt

under warm bands of light
streaming in through arched windows
I say my own farewell

Serey and Samnang pick me up at noon
and I climb into the backseat
and don't tell them about the aunt—
I need a rest from all that ache

in the front seat Serey is friendly and funny
turning to chat and catch up with me
and today that's fine by me

but it's as if we're old friends
as if she has no clue that at least
a few people think I "like" Samnang

on the way we stop to pick up
a plastic jack-o'-lantern to fill
with stickers, a bendy spider
barrettes and hair clips for Zena

for Chea Pen and Leap Sok
we get soft candies and chocolates
but Serey and Samnang
shake their heads at jack-o'-lanterns

why? I say

too creepy Serey says
they look like heads
or devils

we sign in at the Newall Center
visit the men first
and there's a sign on their door that says
No Costumes! No Masks! PTSD

PTSD? I say

post-traumatic stress disorder Serey says
and I'm relieved that I was so
distracted by Madoka's aunt
that I didn't make up my face
green and wear a witch hat
like I'd thought to do

Chea Pen and Leap Sok are surprised
to see us on a Sunday
and with all five of us in the room
it's like a party

Serey and Samnang give the men
small bags of Cambodian
and American sweets
and some banana cake from Lily

I take pictures
of Serey and Samnang
with Chea Pen
then with Leap Sok
and tell them I'll print copies

then we go to Zena's room
where the door is nearly closed
so I knock and start to push it open
but I pause because there is a girl there
                    sitting in a chair beside Zena's chair

I say *hi, sorry to interrupt*
then to Zena
I have something for you
is this an okay time?
and Zena looks up

I introduce myself to the girl
and say that I work with Zena on her poems
and she says oh, *the new poet*
I'm Sarah, Zena's daughter
my aunt couldn't come

and I try not to look so surprised
I had no idea Zena had a daughter

Samnang and Serey introduce themselves
and I look at Zena and say
your daughter is beautiful, like you

Zena looks up, then toward the letter board in Sarah's hand
and I watch Sarah, too slowly
like she doesn't do this often
run through the colors and letters
for Zena to spell *c-o-l-l-e-g-e* . . .

Sarah rolls her eyes
I'm supposed to brag to you that I go to BU
and I'm studying public health . . .
then she squints hard at me
I thought you were supposed to be from Japan

I am I say *lived there nearly all my life*

Samnang goes out for another chair
so I can sit beside Sarah
Serey sits on the edge of Zena's bed
Samnang leans against the windowsill
and we chat and Zena seems to glow
with all the company

I hold up the plastic pumpkin
and the paper bag and say to Zena
Happy Halloween!
I brought your costume—
do you want to try it on?

Zena looks up and growls
so I set the pumpkin on her table
take the costume from the bag
and Serey helps me place the half camisole
over her blouse
then Sarah helps arrange the purple satin
over her legs
and I fan the mermaid's tail
over her feet
and finally I pin the shell barrette
in her hair

Zena looks awesome
and Sarah is laughing and clapping
did you make that? you MADE it?
and Serey pushes the chair
before the mirror
and Zena looks up so much
she's crying

I wipe her tears with a tissue
and we take pictures
      me with Zena
      Zena with Sarah
      me with Zena and Samnang and Serey
      Serey with Zena
      Samnang with Zena
and then we get an aide to take pictures of all of us
before wheeling Zena out to the nurses' station

in the hallway
everyone we pass
claps
and gives her a *wow!*
or *way to go, Zena!*
and Zena's face is stuck
in that broad grin

I'm holding the letter board ·
and she spells
39
and Samnang and I
glance at each other
and smile

when we leave it's 1:30
and Samnang and Serey
have to be at dance by 2:00
so I tell them to go on
I'll get a bus
            or walk
                        or call my grandmother or father

Serey looks at Samnang
and raises her eyebrows
and when Samnang lifts his chin
she says *why don't you join us?*

where? dance practice? I ask

yeah, you can watch
then come out with us after

no, no, I don't want to be in the way
and I mean not so much
at the practice
as afterward

but Samnang says
come on
then I'll give you a ride home
around six

so finally I say okay
and from inside the car
in my place in the backseat
on the way to Lowell
I call YiaYia's

Dad answers and I realize
this is a mistake, me going out
considering Mom is recovering
considering everything

but he says *go ahead, you need a break, have fun*
just text me when you're leaving Lowell and . . .
he drops his voice
call if you need me to come pick you up

then I wonder
        if this is a drinking thing
        but somehow with Samnang I seriously doubt it
then I wonder
        if it might be just Samnang and me leaving Lowell
        but somehow I seriously doubt that, too

on the way into Lowell I ask
so who will be there?
and Serey and Samnang name the other dancers
how long they've been with the troupe
who are the strongest dancers
who teaches younger kids now
who dances with other dance groups
and how the director is the grandson
of a royal dancer and that he taught dance
in the refugee camps

they ask about me and dance
so I mention ballet with Madoka
the studio where I'd just started hip-hop
the *yosakoi* dance team I joined
and the *soran bushi* dance with movements
of hauling fishing nets and tossing fish
and I promise to show them videos sometime

then I tell Serey she should show Zena
her mermaid dance sometime

and at the exact same moment
Serey and Sam say *yeah!*

Chapter 30

Fishing Dance

Samnang parks
we walk to the dance center
        an old brick building
            once a boardinghouse for mill workers
and climb up a few flights of stairs

we weave through little kids
and even though they're speaking English
it's like suddenly I'm somewhere in Asia

someone tugs on my sleeve
says *hello!* and it's Lily
surprised to see me there
are you going to dance?
I tell her I'll just be watching

Van is head-butting her
and Lily scolds him in Khmer
while Lena waves to me with one hand
her arms wrapped around Serey

have fun! Lily says
we're leaving now
kids' class is done
but hey, when will you cook Japanese for us?
and I laugh
soon! I say, and think
once Mom is better
we'll have a Japanese night

Serey leads me to the director
tells him I'm from Japan
a friend of Samnang's
and I do *sompeas*

may I watch? I ask
he says *sure!*
follows us to a large room
and brings a chair for me
you want to try? go ahead
but I shake my head, say
thanks, not today
noting that not a single
non-Asian dancer
is assembling
in that studio

soon Serey says *hey, everyone*
this is Emma
she goes to Samnang's school
she's going to watch
so, anyway, be nice to her

they practice the fishing dance
like we saw on the DVD
of Samnang's performances
they don't use basket props
or wear costumes
but I recognize the movements
the boys circling the girls
the flirty advances by the boys
the rebuffs by the girls

they work on some movements
one dancer leading them all
then they turn on the music
and God, I so want to join in
I'm so reminded of *soran bushi*
and some of the dances
we do in the shrine yard
near our house during Obon

I watch Samnang and Serey
and the others
their hands
their expressive fingers
the way they turn
tilt their heads
move their eyes

and again I am filled with envy
that makes me ache for Japan
all these kids moving together
sharing their culture, their background

here in Massachusetts
it seems only Toby, my parents and I
share my background
and what I thought
was my culture, too

if we don't go back to Japan this year
will I lose it all?
my *nakami*—
my filling?

after the fishing dance
they work on another folk dance
the coconut dance, Serey says
though today they don't have
coconuts in their hands

in smaller groups
they do classical pieces
the music slower
then a teacher enters
speaks to them in Khmer
and soon it is Serey and Samnang
dancing together

and I can see right away
      they are an amazing couple
      their backs arched
      their knees outturned
      their eyes connecting
      bodies sliding around one another
      the flow so
            natural

Chapter 31

Americans

when we leave the dance center
the sky is going purple
cold is setting in

we head down the sidewalk
a loose and trailing group
and they're all talking
in small clusters together
and I feel like an outsider
wishing I were an insider

I'm saying a few words
to a girl called Nary
attempting conversation
when a couple stops me
asking for directions

I'm not from here I say
and turn to Nary
who asks Serey

Serey explains to the couple the way
to the street and restaurant they want
then the woman thanks Serey and says
where are you from?

here, Lowell, I'm Cambodian

and the woman says
oh, I thought so!
all cheerful
*you're much too pretty
to be American!*

I bristle
but Serey smiles, polite
and the couple goes away
then after a minute I say to her
you know, you can speak up
say something
when people say stupid stuff like that

she rolls her eyes
says *right*
easy for you to say

and it's hanging there between us
that I'm a white girl

one of the guys
calls out to her
and she jogs on ahead
while I slow

Samnang drops back
to walk with me
you okay?

fine I say
lagging on purpose
but he slows, too
matches my pace

when the others are ahead
he takes my hand
gives it a shake
and says *hey*

I look at him puzzled
stop walking
he's still holding my hand

without thinking I say
Samnang, I don't know what your heys *mean*
and I don't know what this means
looking at my hand in his

he drops my hand
and I think I've blown it
with my only friend here in Massachusetts
by my big fat blathering mouth

he shrugs
we start walking again faster
so the others don't keep looking back
as we head to the cars

before we catch up I say
I'm sorry
it's been a hard week
and I just blurt stuff
when I speak English

no problem he says
but take it easy
just have fun today, okay?

so I decide to do that
just have fun

he says *come on*
and I follow his lead
and we run ahead
to unlock Chris's car

I climb into the backseat
Serey is up front next to Samnang
with a girl named Kanya on her lap
squeezed in with me are Sovann, Nary and Paul
and the others all cram into a different car

everyone's laughing
and finally I am, too
and Samnang drives slow
and super carefully
the short distance
to the restaurant

which is Cambodian

and I am in heaven
as we drink tea
and eat little lort noodles
and papaya salad
and soup which is like curry
that I pour on my rice

and the whole time
Samnang is sitting next to me
not Serey
and she doesn't even seem to mind

before we leave
I take the restaurant's card
and slide it into my wallet

later I will place it in the box
that Gramps made
as my first real American treasure

Chapter 32

Maybe Couple

after we eat and I've had
like seven cups of tea
around six o'clock
just as Samnang promised
we leave

he drives around neighborhoods
dropping people off
finally Serey, too
then it's just us in the car
quiet
as we drive out of Lowell
past the huge homes
of the former mill owners

Samnang says ·
sorry it's a little late
you must be worried about your mom

yeah, a bit I say

but in truth this whole evening
has been a vacation
from worrying about my mom

after a pause
I can't help myself from asking
just to set things straight—

so
how long have you and Serey
been going out?

and I hold my breath

going out? he says
we're not

ex-girlfriend then? I say

not really he says
everyone in the dance troupe . . .
we're friends
like family, you know?

but I think back and say to him
that night your mom made dinner
at Chris and Beth's
she said something about Serey

Samnang waves a hand dismissively
my mom thinks Serey and I are a couple
or a maybe couple
or a could-be couple
'cause I took her to the prom last year

and I'm thinking prom?
ex-girlfriend wasn't far off

well, are you? I ask
a couple?

Samnang sighs
shakes his head
my mom wishes it
and Serey and I sometimes fake it
because Serey has a boyfriend
from the community college
that her parents don't know about
so it helps her get out of the house
if she goes with me

and now I'm totally baffled
you fake it? you pretend you're together?

he nods

do Beth and Chris know you aren't?

he tilts his head
I don't know

what about the other dancers?

Samnang says
oh, they know Serey has a boyfriend
and it's not me

we come to YiaYia's street
and Samnang stops at the corner
then doesn't proceed—
he's looking at me

you're going back to Japan, right?

I nod

January, right?
that's what your grandmother said
the day you had the migraine

I try to read the meaning in his eyes
lit by dashboard and street light

I think we'll be here the full year
my parents don't say anything
about January anymore

Samnang says
you want to go back?

and I say *well, yeah, that's my home*
and after the earthquake and tsunami
I just feel like I should be there helping out
like it's wrong to be here

I tell him about Madoka's aunt
                just found
and her cousins
and their destroyed schools
I'd be more useful in Japan I say

I hear you he says
then shifts in his seat
well, tell your mother and everyone
hello and I hope she recovers fast

and it's not till after I get out of the car, wave
and he's driven off that it occurs to me
                when he asked if I want to go back
                there was another way
                I could have answered
                like I derailed a conversation
                that could have been

Chapter 33

Daughters and Sons

Mom is able to walk a bit
the next day
and after school
I help her take small steps
up the sidewalk
as far as the stop sign
then back again
down the street
on the other side

after that
she's exhausted
but it's warm enough
for her to sit on a lawn chair
wrapped in a blanket
with a cup of hot *yuzu* tea
bathing in the afternoon sun
before it starts to drop

I sit with her
but she doesn't let me stay still for long
insisting that since she can't work I should
she makes me grab a rake from the garage
and rake leaves into piles for YiaYia
        which I do

but Mom tells me I don't rake right
don't put enough strength into it
don't know what I'm doing
        which is true

well, duh, I want to say
I was raised in Japan with yards
so small we picked the leaves out by hand
        but I don't

I'm sweating
shedding layer after layer
scarf, jacket, sweatshirt
as I make a huge pile of leaves
beside her chair
so she can smell them
and reach down
to touch them

the colors are more intense
in Vermont she says

and I wish we could see Vermont
before the leaves drop
before the snow

a little later she gets chilled
I help her inside, get her set up on the bed again
then find Dad who shows me how to rake the leaves
onto an old sheet and carry the bundle
over my shoulder to a compost pile

Dad is here till the weekend
Gram and Gramps staying nearby
cousins and old friends
of Mom's and Dad's drop by
and YiaYia's house is full of traffic
our meals noisy
though Mom is often
too exhausted to join us

there is not much time
to think of poems
or even scribble
in my journal
but sometimes like a meteor
a streak of thought
or a poem line
       shoots through my head

but by the time I open
my journal
late at night
       it's vanished

when I see Samnang at school
I try to stop to talk
say more than *hey*
even though there isn't time
between classes
for much more than *hey*

I ask him about the school dance club
if he's friends with anyone in it
if he knows Tracy or Claire or the two guys
but although he danced with some of them once
he doesn't know anyone well

we make plans to have pizza
after our work at the Newall Center
on Wednesday

but it turns out that Wednesday
is Gram and Gramps' last dinner with us
before they return to Vermont
and I'm supposed to come straight home
after seeing Zena

I beg
offer to get up early
for a farewell breakfast
tell Dad and YiaYia I'll be back
in time for dessert

but there is no getting out of this one
Samnang can come here Dad says
when I explain the pizza plans

I think on that
but say
never mind
it's okay

Wednesday I take the bus to the Newall Center
since Samnang has a gymnastics team meeting
and will be late

Zena's not in her room
so I grab the letter board I prefer
not the one hanging from her chair
and an aide tells me she's waiting
in the library downstairs

where she is
but so is another woman
leafing through a magazine

Zena spells that it's *o-k*
but I feel strange
without privacy

I read Zena a mermaid poem
by Kim Addonizio
from the point of view of a mother
watching
dreaming about
and thinking of
her fifteen-year-old daughter

I say I was searching for mermaid poems
but more than the mermaid
I really liked the metaphor
of the girl's face as a lure
that pulls the mother
from her darkness

next I read aloud the one
by Naomi Shihab Nye
about the mother who tells the daughter
            you know you're going to die
            if you can no longer make a fist

I look at Zena's hands
clenched immobile atop her always folded arms
and tell her *you're fine—you've got good fists*

I tell her I like the line in this poem about
the girl grown up
still lying in the backseat as an adult
behind her questions

I tell Zena I chose these poems
because they had a mother and a daughter
one poem from each perspective
and in each the mother or the daughter
is the other's lifeline in a way
and because of her window poem
about the family posing for a photograph
and because of meeting her daughter on Sunday

but then the woman across the room
the woman who's been leafing through magazines
startles us by saying
I had two sons—
if I'd had a daughter
she'd come see me

I nod, say *well* . . .
and ask Zena if she'd like to write a poem
about being a mother or a daughter
or a mermaid or whatever
and Zena looks up
and I ask the woman with the magazine
if she wants a piece of paper
to try a poem, too
but she says *no, no*
I just have sons

and even though I explain
that she can write a poem
about her sons
or about being a mother
or being a daughter
she still says *no*
I just have sons

I ask Zena if she wants to use
the computer attached to the chair
but she insists on the letter board
so I go down the list of colors
and start spelling Zena's poem
which doesn't have a title yet

letter by letter
word by word
Zena spells
like this poem was just
sitting in her head:

my stroke beached me like a whale on hot sand
come home! my daughter called and called
but I couldn't answer and finally she swam away

by the time I could look up to talk
and tell her to lean over my face
so I could feel the tickle of her hair
she no longer felt like my daughter

come back! I called and called
but she swam away
with my sister

it takes several minutes
staring at Zena's words
for me to comment

Sarah was raised by your sister?
Zena looks up

and I try to grasp
Zena's losses
                movement, speech, her child

I ask how old Sarah was
when Zena had her stroke—
she looks up at 6

I suck in my breath
try to imagine Sarah growing up
with her mother in the care center

what about your husband? Sarah's father? I dare ask

l-e-f-t she spells
2 m-o-n-t-h-s a-f-t-e-r

I try to hold my tongue
but can't help saying *jerk!*
and Zena looks up

but it's great that Sarah comes to see you I say

n-o-t o-f-t-e-n Zena spells
then adds
m-o-s-t-l-y o-n-l-i-n-e

online?
well, that's good! isn't it?

and as I recite the colors and letters
Zena spells

s-e-q-u-e-l
s-h-e s-w-a-m b-a-c-k
w-i-t-h f-a-c-e-b-o-o-k

and this cracks me up
and Zena looks up
five times in a row

then the woman with the magazine
says her younger son was on a swim team
and won a medal in the backstroke

I turn back to the poem
and say to Zena
maybe you should call this poem
Beached
Zena looks up
and I write that on top

then I tell Zena that
I have to go, it's late

I've texted Samnang
to say I'm in the library
but he still hasn't come by

I tell Zena to write more poems about her daughter
if she can get someone to help her with her computer
and I suggest to the woman that she write about her sons

backstroke the woman says *not the butterfly*
I smile at Zena and her eyes seem to smile back

Chapter 34

Loss

at room 427
I peek inside and see
Chea Pen's bed empty
made up neat

Samnang motions me in
and with a glance
at the vacant bed says
Lok Ta Chea is in the hospital—
pneumonia

I put my hands together
do *sompeas* to Leap Sok
I'm so sorry I say
I hope your roommate
returns soon
and Samnang translates

then with Samnang not making to leave
I'm not sure what to do

after a while I point to a photo
beside the bed of some ruins
Angkor Wat?

but Samnang points to the painting by the mirror
that's *Angkor Wat*
then at the photo by the bed
this is Wat Banan
the one with the long steps up

ah, I wish we could see that view
I say, and Leap Sok nods
and Samnang nods
but neither speaks

so I ask what they worked on today

Samnang says
a memory from when he was a monk
     most Cambodian boys
     used to become monks for a while
     many still do
and he was talking about studying
and living at a temple for six years
before the Khmer Rouge took power

Leap Sok murmurs something to Samnang
Samnang hesitates then says
he wants me to tell you
it's still important
for Cambodian boys to become monks
even American Cambodian boys
and he wants me to tell you
that I should do it
maybe go back to Cambodia
to Battambang
to do it

oh! I say
but what about school? and dance?

I could do it when school's off
Samnang says
anyway, here in America
you can become a monk
during school break

really? I say
it sounds almost funny
but I nod, solemn
feeling the tension
in the room

Samnang shuffles his papers, stands
Leap Sok looks away

Samnang speaks to him gentle, steady
puts on his jacket

Leap Sok eyes the empty bed
wipes the corner of his eye with his thumb

Samnang sits down again
and I step out
to wait in the hall

later in the elevator I say
Chea Pen's pneumonia—it's that bad?
and Samnang nods
looking worn and tired

I'm really sorry I say

in the lobby we write the time by our names
and Samnang throws the pen down
which bounces off the desk
and he strides out
while I pick it up
from the floor

out in the cold
it's flurrying

and for a moment Samnang
looks mildly cheered
as he holds out his palm
to catch some flakes

then he starts striding
toward the bridge, the pizza place
and I remember and stop

a few paces on
Samnang stops, too

hey I say *I'm sorry*
hating that I have to tell him
but I can't have pizza tonight
it's my grandparents'
last night with us

he stares straight ahead
blows some air out
shoves his hands into his jacket pockets
and starts walking toward the car
so I should just take you home

his voice is so diminished

and although I wasn't intending to
now I say *you're invited to join us*

he doesn't answer

as we reach the car he blurts
they've lost so much
these older Khmer—
family, friends, homes, their lifestyle . . .
you can't imagine what they went through
during Pol Pot . . .

> *Lok Ta Leap lost his father and mother*
> *uncles, cousins, three brothers*
> *his two youngest daughters . . .*

and they had nothing
when they got here
nothing
it's been so hard

so when they're old
here in America
these Khmer
who can't speak much English
who have hardly any relatives left . . .
or have kids and grandkids
so different from them . . .

when they lose someone else . . .
Samnang turns away

I stand nearby
but not too near
give him space

and after a bit I say
Leap Sok is lucky to have you

but Samnang says sharply
I don't think that's called luck
to just have me

he unlocks the car and we get in
and I don't know what to offer
to his silence

other than more silence

when we reach YiaYia's I say
come inside, just for a bit

I tell him that tomorrow
Gram and Gramps return to Vermont
and pretty soon my father
will be back in New York
it's a big family meal
with my mom joining if she can

Samnang rubs his hand
over his face
eyes the clock
tilts his head
okay, sure
and parks the car

I wait while he calls Beth
then we go up YiaYia's walk

YiaYia welcomes him right in
and sets another place
without my asking
and Dad introduces him as
Emma's friend Samnang
dancer and gymnast
and Gram and Gramps throw him questions
about Cambodian dance
which they call the Royal Ballet
going on about the artist Rodin
and his sketches of Cambodian dancers
visiting France
and I'm wondering . . .
how do they know all this stuff
coming from Vermont?

when dinner is served
YiaYia chats with Samnang
about people at the Newall Center
she knew from when Papou was there
Samnang talks soccer with Toby
and Boston Marathon with my mom
he explains his upcoming gymnastics season
and assures my father, yes, he's looking at colleges

he's lively and good to everyone
and I can tell they all like him

but now I know that
even when Samnang is animated
he's still carrying all that loss

after dinner I grab my jacket
go outside with him to the car
and ask if he'll visit Leap Sok
again this week or if I should drop by

I'll try to go he says
but I don't think you should bother
he doesn't speak much English
and it's slurred
from the stroke

I tell him I think I can handle that
I work with someone who can't even speak

he gives a half smile
then says *thanks*
for dinner and everything

and I tell him *anytime*
and out of habit
my head drops
into a slight bow

a little later
when I'm helping YiaYia wash dishes
I get a text:
    39

Chapter 35

Path

when I get home from school on Friday
Dad meets me at the door
and before I can even step inside
he says *let's go for a walk*
we got the path report

and I begin to panic—
they already took off the whole breast
the lymph node tested negative
the tumor was only .3 cm . . .
what's left to report?

it's okay
nothing unexpected
no bad news he says

and as we head down the sidewalk
he goes on to tell me that the surgeon
and the oncologist and the radiologist agree
there's the slightest chance of cancer cells in the chest wall
and that radiation followed by five years of hormone therapy
is considered the best course of treatment at this time

no chemo? I ask
no chemo he says

well, that's good I say
breathing again
relaxing my shoulders

Dad says radiation will start just after Thanksgiving
that it will be five times a week for seven weeks
and that after those seven weeks
she'll start taking tamoxifen
and her body will need to adjust

nothing unusual Dad says

I raise my eyebrows
but I hold my tongue—
this whole year has been nothing but
            unusual

how does this happen to someone who runs? I say
and wears sunscreen
and doesn't eat much meat?
it's not fair

cancer is never fair he says
but lots of women are survivors, Em

he says Mom will be fine but may be tired
from the radiation
and she'll need lots of help
emotional and physical—
YiaYia's help
Toby's help
Dad's help
when he can be there
and especially
my help

she counts on you, Em he says

too much, I think
but don't say

I pause on some bumped-up concrete where
a tree root has cracked open the sidewalk
like a wound

how is she today? I say
but we have to move down the sidewalk
when a leaf blower starts

okay, kind of deflated
resigned, maybe he says

we both know
she's going crazy
without her running

then Dad says *I'm sorry, Em*
but it looks like you and Toby
should just finish the school year here
even if I have to go back to Japan sooner
which, you know, I probably will
maybe in winter

I take a deep breath
and stare across
a long sloping yard
dotted with Canada geese

and I'm thinking
what if *I* went back with Dad . . .

but then I think of Zena's poem
of her daughter
swimming off with her sister

and how if I went back with Dad
wouldn't that be like
abandoning Mom?

I tell Dad *don't worry*
I'll help Mom get back on her feet

he says *thanks, Em*
I know you will

we walk back to the house
but before checking in with Mom
I tell him I need to go for a run

I put on some sweats
and dash back outside
to get my head in order
so I don't blurt
the wrong words to Mom

I don't even stretch
just start running
and right away I'm aware
I don't have enough layers
for this frigid New England air

I launch into a sprint
bolt down my usual route
then keep going straight
where I'd usually loop right
pushing, pumping, straining
as if I want
        to feel a muscle tear

when I slow my pace finally
I try to list what this all really means

1. my mother still needs treatment
2. Dad won't be with us much
3. I'm staying in Massachusetts for a full school year
4. I won't get back to Japan until way after
   the one-year anniversary of the quake

as I reach mile three
I'm relieved the list is only
four points long
that I can start to mull or stress
as YiaYia might say
on just those four points

my body finally warms
and I even have to walk
awhile to cool down
when I reach YiaYia's
at dusk

my mother's in an armchair
with a lap desk and her computer
which she closes when I sit
down on the edge of the bed

cancer sucks I say

sure does she says
but I'm not alone, Em
about 12% of women in this country
will get breast cancer
and this is all standard treatment
precautionary, okay?
I nod, encouraged to see
that glint of determination
returning

then she says
I love that I can always count on you, Em

and though it's meant as praise
it feels like a weight
transferred
strapped
to my back

Mom gazes out the window
to tree limbs bathed in streetlight
and sighs
I wish we were in Japan she says
I miss my running routes, my students . . .
I can get enough America when I'm in Japan
but I can't get enough Japan when I'm here
and this year, of all times, to have to leave . . .

I want to agree
add my own rant to hers
but instead I say
yeah, but we'll get back home soon enough
and you'll run those same routes
probably faster

she looks away
purses her lips
and I know she's fighting tears
and I need to change the subject

we sit in silence for a while
then I say what's clear to me now
I'm thinking that somehow
I have to help Tohoku from here

and after a moment
she says
really? me, too
let me know if there's
something I can do

and I realize I'll need to give her
an assignment
because she has to get her mind off
her own body

I glance around the crowded room
that used to be YiaYia's sewing room
now cluttered with Mom's stuff
will we stay here?
at YiaYia's the whole year?
we won't move to Vermont?

we'll stay here she says
near the hospitals and clinics

well then I say
if you'll be an adviser
for my Tohoku project
I'll cook you Japanese food

deal! she says
then she whispers *poor YiaYia!*

and I laugh and she laughs
until she hurts and grimaces
and I make us both banana yogurt smoothies
with protein powder and *yuzu* preserves

and while we're sipping the smoothies
even though I feel like
one of those surfers the helicopters
hover over Sagami Bay searching for—
  a surfer being sucked out to sea
  tumbled and plunged
  under typhoon waves higher
  than anticipated

we bounce ideas back and forth
for helping people in Tohoku
from here in Massachusetts

after I finish my homework
I sit on my bed with my journal
and fiddle with a list

    in a year the snowcap
    grows to a full skirt
    then recedes
    a breast disappears
    the cat grows fatter
    kanji go fainter
    temple bells gong
    a father shifts jobs
    a boy loses language
    a mother stops running
    rubble is cleared
    a body is found
    incense is burned
    houses repaired
    and a daughter
    doesn't know what to do

I think of Miyagi
and how much is gone

I think of Madoka's aunt
so long unfound

I think of Samnang's mother
and all that she endured

I think of my mother

I think of Zena

and I wonder
what to do

Chapter 36

Seeing the Buddha

Saturday Dad drops me at the Newall Center
while he goes out to find an Asian market
to shop for groceries—
        comfort food and ingredients
        that he thinks Mom may want
        but YiaYia won't know to buy:
                soba noodles, miso, tofu, ginger, nori

first I stop in to see Zena
and find her in her room
working on her new computer
writing with the eye tracker

I ask how it's going and she looks up
then she starts typing a line to show me
the slow and deliberate process
choosing letters to type
or selecting words
from the prompt list
all with a blink

then she spells
h-o-w r u?
turning the conversation
on me

okay I say
then she spells for me to turn her wheelchair
and when I do Zena looks right into me
and points with her eyes toward a chair for me

I pull the chair up beside her
and I feel so pathetic sitting there
before a paralyzed woman
who can't move her arms or legs
who can't speak
and whose daughter
had to be raised by her sister

but I can't help it
tears come
I wipe them away
try to calm myself
taking three slow breaths

sorry I say to Zena
I act all put together for my parents
but I seem to have no control
over anything anymore

Zena points her eyes at the letter board
but first I stand up for a tissue
then sit down again
and to Zena's questions
I explain Mom's treatment
our staying for a year
and that though it's not
what I'd hoped for
I'll try to make it work

I run my finger over the letter board
which can still be faster than her computer

Zena spells
t-a-k-e c-o-n-t-r-o-l o-f w-h-a-t u c-a-n
l-i-k-e m-e

I thank her
tell her I'll try
then pull Mom's computer
from my bag

I open Mom's laptop to my slide show
tell Zena I brought something to share
with Samnang's Cambodian patient
but I can give her a quick viewing

there's not much time
Dad will be back soon
but her eyes go bright
as I click through

when I have to leave
she spells *n-e-x-t t-i-m-e m-o-r-e*
and I promise her *of course*

Leap Sok's dozing
but he wakes, and while aides
get him dressed in fresh clothes
I step out into the hall

when I go back in I do *sompeas*
even try *chum reap sour*
then use simple English and gestures
give him slices of YiaYia's pumpkin bread
feed him bites I tear off
bring water to his lips
and tell him I brought some pictures

I open Mom's laptop
set it on the overbed table
and click the right arrow
to view the slide show

I show him
photos of Kamakura
the main shrine
the lotus ponds
the hills
the big Buddha
temple gardens
samurai tombs
the beach
our house
Madoka
my middle school
my little room
     that overlooks a neighbor's loquat tree
and Shoga
     curled up on my bed

he says *good, good*
so nice, yes, nice
but then he says
something
I don't understand
until he repeats—
tsunami?

photos of the tsunami areas? I ask

and he nods

so I take a deep breath
go to the photo files
and pull up pictures
from the cleanup

but flipping through
seeing those bashed
and shredded neighborhoods
brings back all that pain

and I think
        what
        am I doing?

I return to my original plan
and play a video Dad took last fall
from the ridge by our house
of the sun going down
behind mountains opposite
        and the surfers at the beach
        and Mount Fuji's new snowcap
        and the chimes playing
        the sunset song

when it's time to leave
I give Leap Sok
a postcard of the Kamakura Buddha
set it on his dresser
near the Angkor Wat painting
and with my hands
do *sompeas*

he nods
eyes the Buddha
says *thank you*

Dad picks me up
and we run errands
for practically the rest
of the day

and finally
on the way back to YiaYia's house
I say to him *I'm going to try*
to raise money for Tohoku
I think long term they'll need help
PTSD and all

definitely he says
and funds for repairs
and programs
and revitalization . . .
so what's your plan?

I tell him maybe
something with dance
but whatever it is
I'll give Mom a role

and he likes that

after dinner I scribble some ideas
to share with the school dance club
and some to share with Samnang
then I start hearing a poem

finally I take out my journal
and focus

Kamakura Buddha with Leap Sok

I'm seeing the Buddha I've been photographed with
every year since the year after I was born
the Buddha whose bronze knees I've sat beneath
the Buddha whose cast insides I've touched
the Buddha exposed in 1498 by a tsunami
the Buddha that sits century after century
the very Buddha that I will not be photographed with
on my birthday this coming January

he's seeing that Buddha
a Buddha he's never known
seated before hills he's never seen
blossom or go green

but in his eyes
I see he's seeing the Buddha
and recognizing the Buddha
he knows

that night I text Samnang—
I need to talk to you about dance

and

know any good Cam poems in English? for Zena?
because I'm thinking that I'd like to read some
and she might, too

and he replies
okay to dance talk
no to poems, but can check

and I text back
I saw Leap Sok today

then my phone rings

you saw him? he says
and I can't help but laugh
that he so did not think I'd do that
how did you talk?

I explain that
I know how to speak
in simple English
and I showed photos of Japan
and even places in Tohoku
after the tsunami
and he's all quiet
just listening
that's amazing
he finally says

but I don't think it's really amazing

I ask if he thinks it was a mistake
to show Leap Sok the photos from
tsunami-hit towns, PTSD and all

nah, tsunami trauma is different
from war trauma

then I say
it looks like we're not moving back to Japan this year
not till summer

Samnang is quiet for a moment
is your mom sicker?

no, no, just radiation therapy
for seven weeks
then hormone treatment
things that take time

oh, well, good he says

yeah, mostly

I mean, I thought you meant
they found more cancer
or she needed more surgery he says

no I say
nothing like that

well, I'm sorry Samnang says
I mean, that you can't go back to help and stuff
'cause I know that's what you want
but in one way it's great

what way? I say

Zena he says

which, it's true
is great
but isn't quite
what I was hoping
he might say

Chapter 37

Seven Times Down

I should have anticipated this one
since it hits post-stress
like clockwork

Sunday
two days after the path report
I'm brushing my hair
when I note a finger of my hand
        missing
then from my face in the mirror my left eye
        missing
and from the window in my room an entire pane
        missing

I haven't even had breakfast
I have tons of homework
I've already had a full night's sleep
I don't want to sleep more
but there's nothing I can do
except go back to bed

I put on my pajamas again
swallow my pills
yank the curtains closed
crawl under the quilt
and cover my face with a T-shirt
for dark

now and then I open my eyes
check the migraine progress—
first the spreading blindness
then a flickering crescent
overlaying the blindness

then I don't need sight
to note the progress
as I feel numbness
seep into my arm
advance along my jaw
and slip into my throat

YiaYia comes in and starts telling me
that it's nearly 9:30
she already woke me once
and got me out of bed
but I press my hands
over my eyes
whimper
and she says *oh!*
tiptoes out
then tiptoes back
with a bottle of water

later Dad comes in
and sits on the edge of my bed

this is his day to leave for New York
but now that it's time to say good-bye
I can't make sense of his words
can't form sentences
language jumbles
I hear

       mother

     radiation

   walk   *Toby*

     Yia   *in the*

support

   school

     you *run*

            love you

and only with effort
can I mutter
two words together
  thank *you*

I feel him kiss my pounding head

tears dribble from my eyes
squeezed shut
against any hint of light

and then in the darkness
behind my closed eyes and amid
the flickering lights and my aphasia

there is playing out in my head . . .
music
and I see with such clarity
hip-hop moves
and the *soran bushi* dance
and the *tanko bushi* dance
and flowing circles
of people all ages
dancing
raising money
for Tohoku

it's early afternoon when I rise
in the foggy afterwards
and slowly pad downstairs
sit at the kitchen table
and drink some tea
that YiaYia sets before me

Mom sits down opposite
oh, sweetie she says
I'm so sorry if my situation
is too much for you

I manage a smile, say
it's okay
even though I feel
like a train wreck

I feel empty of all that energy
I had before the migraine
during the migraine

I chew the chicken salad sandwich YiaYia makes for me
but it tastes like bland mashed baby food
what I'd love is an *onigiri* with salmon or ume
what I want is a hot bowl of soba noodles
topped with sesame and *kizami* nori
what I want is a cup of green tea, not Lipton
what I want is to go home

suddenly I'm not so sure I can handle
my big dance-club fund-raising idea

I put my head down on my arms
by my plate
on the kitchen table

but then the doorbell rings

it's Samnang
and I'm in my pajama sweats
plus a fleece top and slippers
and my hair's all over the place
and YiaYia walks him right
into the kitchen

hey he says to me
and when YiaYia gestures
he sits down at the table
between me and Mom
and YiaYia pours him
a cup of tea

I want to crawl away
and brush my hair
and clean my teeth

but Samnang doesn't seem to care
just talks to YiaYia
and my mom
like it's an everyday occurrence
to drop in

they leave us alone
and I explain about the migraine
and in his eyes
I read concern

Samnang speaks softly
like he knows sound hurts me
says he brought me a book
sets it on the table

the cover has a grim painting
but a subtitle says it's poetry
of Cambodian refugee experiences

he flips through and says
they're long
but maybe you can read some of these poems
to Zena

then he has to leave for dance
feel better he says

I go to the porch with him
and wave when he drives off

and I realize in the surprise of his visit
my head full of the murky afterwards
and refugee poetry
I forgot to mention dance

and then it comes back to me
the whole program
that I saw so clearly in my migraine—
      hip-hop to kick things off
      soran bushi by dance club members
      more hip-hop
      another folk dance
      then the audience
      in expanding rings
      of *tanko bushi*
      to finish up
but now in real time
post creative migraine burst
the program seems too short

I shower
and while I'm under the hot water
I think about staying the full year
> I can go to Vermont in winter
> I can do Model UN in Boston
> I can work with Zena for longer
> I can create a Dance for Tohoku project
> and maybe learn Cambodian dance
> and at least be friends with Samnang

and I realize I'm starting to feel positive
and even when I think of Madoka, and her family
the guilt that runs through me is diluted
knowing I'm going to help from here

I do homework for the rest of the day
counting the hours till tomorrow
when I can find Samnang at school
to ask him, what if
> a non-Cambodian wanted to learn
> Cambodian dance

right before I go to sleep
I remember the book
and I read one of the long poems
that tells the story of refugees at the border
tricked by Thai soldiers into crossing
back into Cambodia
bullets chasing them
land mines in front of them

and I think of the Japanese proverb
七転び八起き
nanakorobi yaoki
seven times fall down, eight times get up

but for Cambodian refugees
        facing land mines
        and bullets
        starvation and disease

and for tsunami survivors
        facing radiation
        and typhoons
        sunken land and floods

I think it's more like
百転び百一起き
hyakukorobi hyakuichioki
a hundred times fall down
a hundred and one times get up

Chapter 38

Tanko Bushi

at school the next day
I look for Samnang in the halls
but don't see him anywhere

at Model UN
Jae-Sun cheers
when I say I'll probably be staying
the full year

then Monica suggests
we all go skating next weekend
at some rink that has public hours

but I've only skated a couple times in my life
at the rink in Yokohama by the Red Brick Warehouse
and I swear I can still feel the bruises

so I just say *maybe*

Jae-Sun appears at my locker
and walks with me to the bus
talking all about New York
and the conference
and his cousins there
and K-Town where the Korean food
is best and how he'll take me there
someday

I'm not sure
what that's supposed to mean
or how I feel
about this attention

on Tuesday at lunch I find Tracy
and tell her my idea
for Dance for Tohoku
and there in the noisy cafeteria
I think she'll dismiss it
as incompatible with the club
but she listens, then suggests
we move into the courtyard
where it's quieter

and then she says
well, a full program
takes a long time to prepare
so I don't know, maybe we could try
to do it by March 11 . . .

and I'm thinking
        not till then?
but fortunately I hold my tongue

because next Tracy says
in the meantime
maybe we could do that tanko bushi *circle thing*
at pep rallies or halftime at basketball games
you know, get people to come onto the court
put a donation into a collection box then join us in the dance
and maybe we could get someone to promise to match
the donations to encourage more people to join in

and I picture that old Kyushu coal-mining dance
with the moves of shoveling, tossing dirt
pushing the coal cart, wiping the sweat
as a feature of this school's halftime shows
and I think of how people love it at Japanese festivals
how everyone joins in when they hear that song start up

and I laugh
it's so ludicrous
it's perfect
halftime *tanko bushi*

I tell her *that*
would be amazing

I can't wait to tell Samnang
but I haven't seen him around
so I text him to be sure
he's going to the Newall Center
this week
and he replies *maybe not*

I text *u ok?*

but he doesn't answer
even when I text him
again
and again

that afternoon it looks like it might snow
but Mom is determined to "exercise"
so I walk with her up the street
at a pace so slow
I'm chilled to the bone
in the damp cold

she's dragging, has no energy
seems spaced-out and low
barely hearing my dance club news
and when we get back to the house
she's stone-faced and tight-lipped
unenthused about halftime *tanko bushi*
or a program for the one-year anniversary
and I know she's just barely
holding herself together
hating that she can't run
hating that she's not working
hating that although she's healing well
she doesn't feel like her old self

I forget about *tanko bushi*
help YiaYia make dinner
salad and tuna casserole

scarcely able to swallow my quip
about how I don't get why on earth
people eat fish from cans

Chapter 39

Cranes

I finally call Samnang
Tuesday night

what's up? I've texted
like, a hundred times I say

then hear
Lok Ta Chea died
over the weekend
I found out Sunday night

I suck in air
say I'm sorry
but the truth is
I'd forgotten
Chea Pen was in the hospital
will there be a funeral?
should I go?

there's a funeral
and cremation
and a seventh-day ceremony
but you don't need to go
it's all Cambodian he says
and just so you know
tomorrow
the Newall Center
I won't be going
I spent this afternoon
with Lok Ta Leap

oh I say
I'll stop by
to see him

the next day I take the bus
to the Newall Center
and Zena's frustrated
with her computer—
the word predictions
aren't always bringing up
exactly what she wants

give it time I tell her
let's just use the letter board today

and we do
but she's impatient
and irritable
and finally I figure out
that she doesn't have any poems
besides those she's typed
into the computer but can't
seem to retrieve to show me
and doesn't want to spell out
all over again

I consider reading her the refugee poem
from the book Samnang loaned me
but it seems too harsh for her mood
so I read a poem that I found online
written by a performance poet
after her first visit to Phnom Penh
a poem that repeats in a list
and is full of hope
for the children of Cambodia
like the poet herself

Zena looks up when I ask if she likes it
but there's no shine in her eyes
no spark of connection
so I ask if she wants to talk
or write poems
by letter board
or if she'd just rather work on her computer
but she seems exhausted by
her struggle to be able to write
independent of any helpers

so I tell her I'll come to the workshop
led by that poet from the university on Saturday
I joke that this will save me from a skating date

and Zena looks up
a slight gleam in her eye

I tell her I'll bring the notebook
so we can share poems
we've worked on
even if we can't
access the poems
in the computer

she looks up again
but her eyes are heavy
so I get ready to leave

see you on Saturday
I say

I stop by Leap Sok's room
do *sompeas*
and tell him I'm so sorry
and bow

I set my things down
and from my bag I pull
sheets of origami *washi* paper

I fold five cranes
and set them around the room

      on Chea Pen's food table
      by the photo of Wat Banan
      near the Buddha and Angkor Wat
      on Chea Pen's empty bed
      and before a small shrine
            set up on the dresser with
            candles, incense and flowers
            and a photo of Chea Pen

Leap Sok nods
and I bow
and go

then I return to Zena
who's blinking at her computer again
and I put cranes all over her room, too
and even fold a purple one
and tuck it into the barrette in her hair
and finally, finally, finally
her eyes smile

Chapter 40

Ever

YiaYia picks me up
and hands me my
black sweater
black skirt
and some flats
which I change into
in the car

she was the one
who insisted we go
and through Beth reached Lily
who gave her the details
on Chea Pen's funeral

so despite what
Samnang said
about me not needing to go
YiaYia drives us
to the Buddhist temple
where we pay our respects
to Chea Pen and his family

I show YiaYia *sompeas*
on the way in
and she even does it
and holds the incense sticks
and sets them in the pot

everyone is in black and white
and I recognize a Newall aide there
and a dancer from the troupe
and we catch a glimpse of Lily
but not Samnang
before we have to leave

afterward we shop at three different markets
because YiaYia doesn't like supermarkets
long as football fields

then we stop at an ATM in a plaza
with a Whole Foods
and I say *what's that?*
too expensive YiaYia says
but I say *can't we just go in?*

she says *we've finished all the shopping*
but I beg and she says grudgingly
all right, go see what it's like
but just for a minute
then she comes in with me

I gaze at the produce
pick up some shiitake
white and purple eggplant
greens that look like *komatsuna*
and sesame seeds for *ohitashi*

I offer to cook that night
to make rice, *ohitashi*
grilled eggplant with ginger
and salmon done with
soy sauce, sake and lemon
like we make in Kamakura

so YiaYia supervises
and even gives me a few tips
like using white wine since there's no sake
the way to do spinach in a steamer
and how to cook rice
without a rice cooker

Mom brightens
says it's a perfect dinner
and even calls Dad to tell him

on Thursday I still don't see Samnang at school
so I text him in the evening
when I think all the ceremonies might be done
        ask how he's doing
            if he'll join the poetry workshop

but he texts back *I'll pass*
and a few minutes later
adds *I'm seeing my dad Sat*

I text back
your dad? should you?
but he doesn't reply

on Friday night
I text Samnang again *you ok?*
he texts back *for now*

I call him
hey, are you really okay?

yep, doing great
voice low and empty

you're not I say
are you seriously going to see your dad?

yeah he says
and something about the way he says it
makes me uneasy

is that a good idea? I say

I can hear his sharp intake of breath
then I can make out voices, music
people in the background

Samnang! where are you?

some party

are you drinking?

not yet

don't! I say
Samnang, get out of there
just walk out the door and come get me
I'll be outside my grandmother's house

he's silent
but I hear his breathing
and I wait through
five inhales
and five exhales

yeah, okay

Mom is in bed, Toby beside her
they're watching a movie
and I tell her I'm going out
with Samnang for a bit

she pauses the movie
asks Toby to refill her water glass
and when Toby's out of earshot
I say *he just needs to talk*
I'll be back soon
my phone is charged

her eyes are stern

I know it's late I say
but he's a careful driver
and I'll call
if I need someone
to come get me

I put on my jacket, scarf, hat, gloves
and wait at the end of the driveway
jumping up and down and doing arm circles
hoping he really will come

finally I see his headlights
but when I climb in the passenger seat
there's a six-pack on the floor
with one can missing

where's that one? I ask

out the window he says

did you open it?

yeah, then I chucked it at a tree

why'd you open it? I ask

no reason

there's always a reason I say

and I tell him to go somewhere we can talk
instead of driving around
heading nowhere

we park at a diner
go inside
order ginger ales
and french fries

the reason I say *tell me*

he rubs his hands over his face
all through his hair, then says
I don't know
Lok Ta Chea—it hit me hard

I wait
push the fries toward him
he gulps his ginger ale

he starts again
it's just the push and pull of people
that gets to me
some people expect me to
do this
others that
I'm supposed to be
Cambodian one minute
American the next
my elders want this
my teachers want that

I nod
sip my ginger ale
order him another

and sometimes there's this draw to my father
and I want to see him but I know I shouldn't
and I can't seem to separate him from drinking
and I hate the way Beth and Chris and my mom and stepfather
all talk down about him and warn me off him

sometimes I just want a break he says
from all the expectations
people have of me
in Lowell

it's like I can never just chill
there's always something that has to be done
> *for family*
> *for the community here*
> *for people in Cambodia*
there's not much room
for doing what I want

what is it you want to do? I ask

I don't know he says
but I want to figure it out myself

I tell Samnang
what Zena told me
            take control of what you can

and I tell him to call me
if he feels the need to see his father
if it's really just a need to drink
and then I say
I could go with you
to see him sometime
if you want
I could be there, nearby

he says *thanks*
and then he's silent
and I give him more silence
as we go through the pile of fries

the six-pack with one missing
is at my feet as we buckle our seat belts
Samnang turns up the heat
and starts reversing to head out of the lot
but I tell him to drive around
to the back of the diner

when he does I get out
and place the five beers
on the ground by the back door
       an offering

then I jump in the car
say *go!*
and we drive around the front
without being seen

now, take me to Chris and Beth's I say
then I'll have Chris drive me home

but Samnang pulls out onto the main road
going the opposite direction from Chris and Beth's
and says *no*

no?

no he says

why? I say now nervous

I'll take you home first Samnang says
then I'll go home
I didn't drink, I won't drink
so don't you doubt me, too

okay, I won't doubt you

ever he says

and I'm surprised by this word

he glances at me
slows the car
says it again
softly
       ever

and I take a breath and say
       ever

Chapter 41

Workshop

Samnang doesn't go see his dad
and when he and I arrive
at the Newall Center the next morning
chairs and wheelchairs
are already arranged in a circle
and Lin, the rec director
is laughing and chatting with everyone
and I'm beginning, just beginning
to get her jokes

Samnang sits by Leap Sok
I sit by Zena who's grinning
seated as she is in her chair
radiant, in full mermaid costume

Serey's between two Cambodian women
and there are a number of
university students, it seems
paired with other patients

the poet introduces herself
and says how happy she is to be with
          all of us poets
that she can't wait to hear
what we've been working on

she tells us first
we will go around the room
and read, each read
a poem
or a stanza from a poem
or a paragraph or two from a story
or a section from a memoir

and she looks at each of us students
and says *you, too!*

aside from Zena
and my English teacher Mr. Hays
and on birthday cards
I have never shared my poems
with anyone

I lean toward Zena
and read over her shoulder
the page displayed on her computer
a poem *As a Mermaid*
written on her own
with blinks

then we sit
ready

in turn
patients and students
and students for patients
read poems
on all topics—
        a bicycle, storms, fingers, memories
in all sorts of forms—
        odes, haiku, free verse, even a sonnet
and after each one
people clap and *aah*
and sometimes whoop
and Zena sometimes growls
and Serey and Samnang
and Portuguese and Spanish and other language speakers
murmur translations to their patients

Serey reads one woman's memoir scene
about a way to catch fish in a lake
and another woman's list poem
of things learned from her mother

then Serey reads her own poem
an ode to her *kben*
which she explains is the long cloth
that is folded and wrapped around the body
and twisted and pulled
between the legs
to make the loose trousers
she dances in

my stomach flutters
as the turns to read
go around the circle
and approach
Zena and me

when it's Zena's turn I announce to the group
that Zena wrote her poem by herself on the computer
and everyone cheers

I read from the display:

As a Mermaid

wearing the tail
I can swim
not walk
but good enough

wearing the tail
I can repel
mean nurses
and get away

wearing the tail
I can lounge on the rocks
and watch the world
go by

wearing the tail
I can propel
myself forward
to poems

Zena beams her widemouthed smile
as everyone claps and *woots*

then it's my turn
and I release all the air in my lungs
take a huge breath and start

by explaining
that I'm from Japan
was raised in Japan
that I was reading in Japanese
before I was reading in English
and that I just recently moved here
and I'll show them the kanji as I read

then I read my poem:

Lonely Is

when the language outside
is not the language inside
and words are made of just 26 letters
not parts that tell stories

like sun over birth for star 星
or four people under a roof for umbrella 傘
or person and heavy and strength for work 働

when you stare at letters that make up
a word and the letters themselves
are just lines and shapes
that don't tell stories that join
to create the story of the word

like a hiding sun
is dark 暗
like a long road
is far 遠
like a heart a long time
endures 悆

everyone claps
Zena growls

and I turn to Samnang
and he's looking at me funny

your turn I whisper

then Samnang snaps to
and reads for Leap Sok
a Cambodian village memory
in honor of Chea Pen
first in Khmer
then in English

Samnang then
reads his own poem
which he says is maybe not a poem
since he didn't use line breaks

Coins

My grandmother goes to a friend's house for coining. The copper
coin is rubbed over her back. Red lines appear, swell and sting.
The rubbing makes friction. The friction makes heat. The heat
battles the cold inside. So she says in Khmer to me.

Coins drop into a jar. Coins are collected and saved. Coins
are counted and donated. Coins become cash. Cash becomes a
chance for a kid to learn to dance.

In Cambodia no coins were used. I paid with dollars.
Sometimes I received Cambodian riel bills as change. But
no coins. When I helped my village cousin with his English
homework, he practiced his pronunciation. He asked me to
say each word, then said it after me. When we got to the
word coin, he said, "You know—coin"—making a circle
with his thumb and finger—"like you can see in the National
Museum." Then I emptied my pockets and gave him all my
quarters, dimes, nickels and pennies.

after the readings everyone cheers
and the poet says she is moved
by what we have all accomplished

then we talk about journeys
the different meanings of the word
and we brainstorm going around the circle
words that come to mind
when we hear the word *journey*—

airplane
backpack
journal
Puerto Rico
dust
sneakers
hotel
reunion
luggage
sunset
tears
cockroaches
immigration
money
magic carpet
legs Zena says
and I say *Tohoku*

the poet hands out three poems
that are all about travels and journeys
one called "Enough"
in which the journey
vaguely contemplated
has not yet been taken
another by Maxine Kumin
about running away together to an island
and another by Chinese poet Bei Dao
about standing by a boundary
and wanting to cross to the other side

she says to read these poems
again at home
and for next time
to write a poem or memoir
or something
that has something
to do with travels or journeys

and my mind
is already churning
with ideas

Chapter 42

Corner

Samnang, Serey and I
leave the Newall Center together
and I sit in back
as usual

we talk about the poems
and the poets
and we're all jazzed
and I feel like right now
I really, really am lucky

in the backseat I am thinking
I have so much I want to write
and so much more I want to hear—
like, what other poets have to say
and how other poets experiment
and play with words

and now that I know
that everyone
is a poet
or can be a poet
in a way . . .

but I stop thinking poetry
because in the front seat

Samnang is singing along
loud to a Bruno Mars song
and Serey is joining in
and Samnang knows all the lyrics
and whistles
and moves
and he has to slow the car to drive and sing
and do the hand motions
and I nearly pee in my pants
I'm laughing so hard

and I'm so glad to see Samnang
back to himself

after we drive into the center of Lowell
to drop Serey at her house
Samnang turns the car around
pulls over by a curb and says *lunch?*

and I want to say yes
but I say *well . . .* kind of slow
because YiaYia said to come straight back
to watch Toby while she takes my mother
shopping for shirts that aren't tight on her chest

then Samnang says
noodle soup?

and I say
in that case, yes
but then I have to get home

we go to the same restaurant
where we ate with the dance troupe
but this time we take a small table
and I order the Phnom Penh noodle soup
which comes with seafood and meat and stuff
that I like except for the thin slices of
what Samnang calls liver sausage

we have tea
and we don't talk
until we're done slurping and drinking
then Samnang says
thanks for your help last night
that was the worst I've been
in three years

I thought I was too late I say

I'm going to AA tonight he says

good I say
and remind him he can call me
anytime

and he says
I know

I look at him
and he looks straight back at me
      into me
and there's a calm
between us

we are just sitting, breathing
I think we are smiling
with our eyes

and I feel like we just turned a corner
but I don't yet know
what's around the bend

when he pulls up in front of YiaYia's
I ask him if he's going to his
dance practice tomorrow
and when he says yes
I ask if I could maybe join in
from, like, next week
learn the folk dances
just following along in the back if it's okay
and he says he'll talk to the director tomorrow

I know I'm only here for a year
but I'd like to learn what I can

he thinks it's fine
and reminds me
the performance is next Friday
so I might have to wait a week or two
to start

I ask if I can watch his performance
if that's okay with him

and he smiles
shakes his head, says
sometimes Zena's right
you really are a dodo

he peers into my eyes
and again practically right through me
then he leans over
lightly turns my chin
kisses me
and says
yes

Chapter 43

Wish

I'm practically flying
when I get in the house

.   for a minute I just hold still
in the quiet kitchen
breathing

not sure if I should
sit
stand
walk upstairs
or put my arms out
and try to soar
up there

I shout
but no one's home except Toby
on the computer in Mom's room
so I go upstairs and flop onto my bed
delirious

when Mom and YiaYia finally arrive
home from shopping for loose shirts
I'm writing in my journal

I go down to the kitchen
and Mom shows me
first one top with asymmetrical lines
then two loose and billowy
next another smocklike—
and she seems so pleased
and I'm pleased for her
but I'm dying to say
something
about Samnang
to someone
anyone
so when she finally
stops talking about the tops
I'm just about to tell her
that things may have changed
between Samnang and me

when Dad calls

Mom slips into her bedroom
kicks Toby off the computer
and out of the room
and closes the door
and she and Dad have a long
drawn-out conversation
Toby and me trying to catch snippets
from the kitchen

nearly twenty minutes later
Mom comes out
and sits down

YiaYia sets chamomile tea
before her
then me
and Toby's looking from Mom
to YiaYia
to me

and I think
something's wrong

what? I say

Mom tells me
it's my choice—
I can go back
to Japan
in January
if I want
since it looks definite
Dad will go back then

she says she and Toby
will stay with YiaYia
but if I want
I can return to Kamakura
just after winter break
to attend international school

we know that's what you want, honey
she says

I lean back in my chair, say
I thought we needed to stay together
you, Toby, me
for all this
that's what you said in August
that's what Dad's been saying

but Mom says something about the prognosis
being better than she'd initially feared
and adds *I think by January*
I'll be able to manage better
even if we have to be apart for a while

she sets out details:
I'd be on my own a lot
I'd have to cook dinners
I'd have to do laundry
be disciplined about my homework
and on and on
but I only half listen

she's waiting for my response

I think she expected me
to jump for joy
because when I sit there
gripping my mug of tea
caught between
Japan and Massachusetts
stunned to have gotten what
I'd secretly been wishing for
she says *Emma?*

after New Year's? I ask

yes Mom says
just after your birthday—
I refuse to miss that

her jaw sets as she says this
and it occurs to me just then
that she's opposed to the idea
and maybe Dad is, too
but they're offering anyway

I count the months, weeks, days
whatever I'd have here
before I left for Japan

the time I'd have to
try Cambodian dance

the time I'd have leading the *tanko bushi*
at halftime shows

the time I'd have for poetry workshops

the time I'd have with Zena

the time I'd have
with Samnang

and suddenly
it seems like nowhere near
enough

I don't know I say
and Mom and YiaYia both
jerk their heads back in surprise

then I consider . . .
the one-year anniversary . . .
I could be there in Japan
maybe even in Tohoku

I'll mull it over I say
set down my tea
I need to think

I go up to my room
close the door
and lie down on my bed
stiff as a plank

I stare at the ceiling
trying to visualize the pros
to each option, the cons
to each option

in my journal
I make lists
but they're no help

Japan
Dad
Madoka
Tohoku visits
international school
fund-raising
one-year anniversary
Japanese language
spring soccer

Massachusetts
Mom
Zena
Cambodian dance
tanko bushi and full program
YiaYia
Toby
driver's license
Samnang

when there's hardly any daylight left
I put on my coat and gloves
and go outside to sit on the freezing bricks
of YiaYia's steps to the backyard

out there it feels private
in the dark and cutting air

but I can't sit still
so I start pacing
back and forth
across the yard
picking up fallen sticks
flinging them at a tree

I don't know what to do
or how I'm supposed to decide
or what the consequences will be
of choosing one way over the other

at last I call Samnang

hey he says warmly
and I nearly lose my nerve
but I ask him
Samnang, I have to know
why did you kiss me today?

oh he says
and he's quiet a long time
so long a car comes to a pause at the stop sign
turns and continues up the street
lights raking yards as it disappears
and the dusk turns silent again

I kissed you because he says softly

I wait for him to say more

that's it?

no he says
but that's all that needs saying right now

and he's right
I can read the air between us
I could read it all day between us
there's no need for words

thanks I whisper

I walk across the yard
to a woodpile left from when
Papou was alive and well
split logs I can barely make out
in the light from the kitchen window

I sit down on the pile
elbow on one knee
head in one hand
holding Samnang's breathing
close to my ear with the other

I want to weep

Samnang I say
I just learned I can go back to Japan
if I want
not right away
but soon

I hear the air explode out of him

like how not right away? he says

like . . . I'd be able to get my permit

and your license?

not my license
I'd go back with my father
to start school in January

I hear a door bang shut
or a book thrown
then he's wheezing
and I count seven inhales
and seven exhales

yeah, but . . . he says

I know I say

then I tell him I need to walk
for a bit, just think
that I need him to stay on the line
and he agrees

I go around to the front of the house
and make my way up the street
over the cracks and swollen
root wounds of the sidewalk

I like that he's okay with silence
as if he's walking with me
I like that he doesn't feel the need
to fill the quiet every second

look
Samnang eventually says
I get it about being pushed and pulled
and pressure and guilt
but you can help from here

I know I can I say
but now they're saying I can go back
and I don't know what to do
I don't know what's right

well, I can't tell you what's right he says

I know, I'm not asking you to
but Samnang, whichever way I decide
I think I may have to try on the idea
before I make it final

Emma he suddenly says *stay*

he's never spoken to me like this
with my name and a command

why? I ask

he hedges
there are plenty of reasons he says
but the vagueness bothers me

like? I ask, just wanting to hear him say

but then his voice turns sharp
like figure it out! he says
and hangs up

I hide out in my room
till YiaYia calls me down for dinner
which I hardly touch
then I go upstairs to write in my journal
but I end up just staring
at a blank page

the next morning
I get an email from Madoka
who must have heard from her parents
that my father's going back

she says she'll be preparing for high-school entrance exams
she says she'll be busy but we can study together if I like
she says we can have dinner together now and then
but her words are muted
she doesn't say she's pleased
or is waiting for me

I disappear into homework
wishing Samnang would call
but he doesn't

and I can't say I blame him

Chapter 44

Plunging

Jae-Sun is mad at me when I mention
the possibility of my going back, saying
I already committed to Boston Model UN
so why can't I just stay till that's over

you flip-flopped he says

my parents flip-flopped I say

I decide not to say anything to Tracy
until I really know what I'm doing

Samnang is sullen
distant and cool
when we meet
in the halls at school

but by Wednesday
when we drive to the Newall Center
he's thawed some
focusing less on later
and more on now

which is what I want to do
for a change

we skirt the topic of my decision
talk about our classes
our plans with Leap Sok and Zena
even dance

he tells me he consulted the dance troupe director
even checked with the other dancers
and they said I can join the practices
from next week after their performance

he adds *I asked about summers, too*
in case you want to join in
whenever you're back here

thanks I say
             as he parks at the center
so grateful that he's waiting
patient
not pressing me
for an answer
on my decision

we sign in
and elevator up
to the wards
to our patients' rooms

when I reach Zena's room I'm surprised
to find Sarah, unannounced
it seems—a class was canceled
and someone in her program had to drive
to UMass Lowell and Sarah caught a ride

my first thought is disappointment
since I'd wanted to talk through my decision
with Zena, to gauge her reaction
seek her guidance

but now I see that Zena
is frustrated with the computer and Sarah
doesn't know what to do, so I drop my bag
put the good letter board in Sarah's hands
then turn away, shuffle papers
pretending to hunt for my poems

finally Sarah gets
letter by letter
word by word
the simple things
Zena is telling her

that she likes Sarah's haircut
that Sarah looks healthy
but should wear a thicker coat
and *b-o-y-f-r-i-e-n-d?*

Sarah says
yes, he's still with me

then Zena spells *w-e-d-d-i-n-g?*
and Sarah quips *no, I'm still in school, remember?*
a bit more surly than seems fair

so I suggest poems

I ask if Zena has a new one
and she looks up
Sarah hesitates, then pulls a chair over
says *mind if I listen?*
and follows along
as I work with Zena

I run my finger down the colors
and rows of letters
and word by word
Zena grows a poem
that makes my throat tighten

but not until I read it aloud
from start to finish
does Sarah suddenly twitch
with understanding

I read:

Hair

locks around a chubby finger
in her mouth
shaken about
tangled and wild
in my face
when she's in my arms
or deep asleep
on the pillow
beside me

trimmed with my sewing scissors
braided with my fingers
toweled dry by my hands

brushed and combed
dry or wet
salty with sweat
how I miss
her hair

after a moment I say
it's beautiful

and I so want Sarah to dangle her hair
on Zena's forehead or say
yes, amazing or some compliment
but she says *I don't know much about poetry*

I rush to ease the tension, say
well, it's the feelings you have
when you hear a poem or read it . . .
like, to me, her poem is
about both being a mom
and not being able
to be a mom

but there's an awkward pause
that's long even by my Japanese standards
so I tell them I brought poems
and they both look to me with relief

the first is
a long skinny poem
about patience
being wider than
we expect it to be
I give one copy to Sarah
while I read the other
three times to Zena
since meanings
grow clearer to me
after several readings

I don't think it's clear at all
to Sarah though
so I go on to the next one
by Derek Walcott
which is another poem about a fist
this one about a fist around the heart
and falling in love
being like madness
and plunging into the abyss

Sarah seems to like this one
and laughs
and Zena looks up
and growls

then Zena points her eyes at the letter board
and spells
r u p-l-u-n-g-i-n-g?

who, Sarah? I say
and I glance at Sarah
but Sarah nods to me
then looks to Zena
and Zena gazes straight
at me

me?

and Zena looks up

so I smile
trying to be mysterious
but just then Samnang walks in
and Zena growls
and Sarah laughs
and I
can't hide

and I look at Samnang
as he moves a step
toward me
and I say
yes, I think I'm plunging
and Zena looks up
and up
and up

when we cross to the pizza place
Samnang puts his arm around me
and I put mine around him
and we are laughing
because I have told him
what Zena's plunging comment
was all about

and I think
this will be too hard
to leave

Chapter 45

Hanuman

Friday is the performance
and YiaYia drops me off
because there's some PTA
event at Toby's school
so I sit by myself in the crowd
reading each word of the program

when the lights dim
five dancers come onstage
and I recognize the blessing dance
the girls with the silver cups
tossing petals
for peace, prosperity
and health

I wait for Samnang

all through the pestle dance
with Sovann and Paul
beating the long
pestle poles on the ground
and Nary and others dancing
        feet fast
between the poles

all through the
slow and formal fan dance
by the girls

I wait
knowing that like those girls
he has to be
sewn into his costume
that it takes more than an hour
to ready for his role

but finally Serey is there
onstage
alone
in an orange skirt
and gold top
and gold tail
and headdress
as the mermaid
Sovann Machha

she dances
around the stage
in stately circles
and slow one-legged turns
her hands curving through the air

then Hanuman
the white monkey king
appears

and Hanuman is Samnang
and I know this is his first time
dancing this role
before an audience

Samnang follows Serey around the stage
in all her mermaid's glitter
and my heart races for him

he bounds monkey-like
holds his dagger high
approaches her from all sides

and in the end
he wins her over
and cartwheels offstage

after a celebratory coconut dance
there's another classical dance

then for the last piece
Samnang is onstage again
in loose blue trousers
with all the dancers—
it's the fishing dance
with the flirting guys
circling the shy girls
the advances
the rebuffs
the beat
of the bamboo fish traps
on the floor

I love this one
and I am hoping
especially I can
learn this dance

but near the end of the fishing dance
I lose one performer
then another
and when I try to see Samnang
his whole body disappears

I want it to be just
the after-blindness
from someone's flash
or a stage light

but it's not

I sink down in my chair
put on my coat
cover my head
with my scarf

the lights come up
the applause is too loud
people rise all around me
I let them climb over my knees
file out
while I stay in my seat
quiet
hidden

eventually Samnang finds me
when the numbness
is in my jaw
and up my arm
and I'm blind and
the crescent of triangles
is flickering and arcing
        right
           out
             of
          his
         head

hey
he says
knowing

I reach my hand out
he takes it
squats down
kisses my hair
and helps me up
and outside to the parking lot

inside the car I'm shivering
Samnang reclines my seat
blasts the heat
covers me with his jacket
drives

when we stop
he helps me into
YiaYia's house

I hear my mother and Toby
I feel myself led
to my mother's bed in the den
I feel my shoes removed
        by Samnang
my coat removed
        by Samnang
smelling his head
hot, damp and not yet showered
after dance

and I hear some words
        stay

sit

                Emma
        while

.

it seems everyone has left
the voices are farther
the dark is smooth

then the edge of the bed
          dips
and someone is
beside me
with me

Samnang
still
and quiet

he takes my hand

and I curl against him

and sleep

he's gone of course
when I wake in the night
and go out to the kitchen
for some toast which I eat
sitting on the counter
in the ghostly blue streetlight

and in my head I hear
hey

and I think
maybe now
I'll start to know
my life

in the study I find my phone
in my bag on the floor
and from the bed set up for my mom
I call Samnang
wake him
apologize

we murmur
our voices low
both of us half-asleep

you were a great Hanuman I tell him

thanks he says *sorry you got sick*

he tells me he sat and talked
with my mom and Toby after I fell asleep
before YiaYia got home

he tells me Mom asked him
if he knew
what I'd decided
      and he said he didn't
      but he hoped I'd stay
      even though he understood
      that maybe I needed to go
and she said she felt exactly the same

she mentioned a dance project he says
and I realize I haven't told him
my plans for Dance for Tohoku

I close my eyes and tell Samnang my idea
the vision that was so clear
in that creative burst
during my last migraine

my dance program
of hip-hop
followed by *soran bushi*
more hip-hop
a folk dance from Tohoku
then a circle dance of *tanko bushi*
with the audience
all to raise money for Tohoku
and I tell him what Tracy suggested
tanko bushi for halftime shows
then the full program in March

but the full program doesn't feel quite full enough
I say groggily
the program needs more . . . something

then Samnang says soft but so clear
that the words plunge deep into my ear
maybe you should add some other kind of dance
like Cambodian

Cambodian? I say
to raise money for Tohoku?

yeah, like the fishing dance
or the monkey dance

I don't get it I say
how does that relate to Japan?

well, in the villages where my relatives live
tons of things were funded by Japanese NPOs—
> *schools, wells, irrigation systems, even some of the houses*
you could mix in Cambodian dance
Cambodian dancers raising money, too
as a kind of thank-you to Japan

I take this in
what he's saying
my eyes wide open now
you mean, like, some members of your troupe
plus the school dance club
performing together?

why not? he says

and I smile
there on my mother's healing bed
in my grandmother's den
holding the voice of Samnang
close to my ear

that
would be amazing I say

yeah he says

but Samnang I whisper
if we did that
we'd have to start practicing soon
to be ready for the one-year anniversary

and I hear his breath catch
as he calculates
that date

Chapter 46

Plum Island

I sleep late
shower
eat cereal
and finally
call Madoka
midnight
her time

turn on Skype
I tell her
please

when I can finally see her on the screen
seated at her desk
face brightened by her study lamp
her favorite sax-player posters
      Sadao Watanabe, Kaori Kobayashi and Mindi Abair
barely visible in the dark behind her

I take a long breath and say
I won't be coming back with my father
there are too many reasons to stay—
my mom, Zena, dance
Samnang . . .

she smiles, wearily, says it's okay
she hadn't expected I would
and had worried that I actually might
even though I shouldn't

when I squint at her, puzzled
she elaborates
just take care of your mother
that's your obligation now

and I marvel at how in just a couple months
my thinking seems to have shifted slightly
like a fault slip in an earthquake
away from Madoka's clear-cut view of life
with obligation guiding everything
and I'm glad that I made this decision
not just by ranking my obligations

maybe I have
become a little more of an
amerika-jin

but Miyagi I say
your relatives need so much help
your grandparents, your cousins, those towns
up and down the coast of Tohoku . . .

Emma she says
it's just a half year or so, right?
and besides, other people are helping, too
that's everyone's responsibility, not just yours

well, tell your cousins
I haven't forgotten them I say
and that I'm starting a project
to raise money for their schools
so we'll want to know what they need—
can you ask them to make some lists?
talk with their teachers, start thinking
of what they might purchase
with funds we raise?

I explain my dance idea—
Tracy's crazy suggestion
of *tanko bushi* at halftime
and the full Dance for Tohoku program
for the one-year anniversary

Emma-chan, sugoi!—great!
they need so much she says
            band instruments, sports uniforms, cameras . . .
everything was swept away

then she tells me about the service for her aunt
changes in her grandparents' town
and the plans for rebuilding

we'll do what we can to help I say

after we end our Skype
I shut myself in my room
and make a card
using the outline of a runner
I find on the Internet
shaped a bit like my mother
traced again and again
to create a woman speeding
across the page

inside
I write my message
with my revised poem

a healing breast
on a running woman
is hardly noticed

early afternoon I give my mother the card
and I tell her I look forward
to being her pacer
when she starts running again
in spring

and suddenly she's bawling
like she hasn't ever let herself cry
through any of this cancer mess

YiaYia comes running
followed by Toby
and at first they wonder
what I did now
to upset Mom

but I tell them my decision
and Toby does this new high five
he's been trying to teach me
and my mom smiles through her tears
and YiaYia hugs me tight

then I call my father in New York
and he is so relieved
he sounds like he might cry, too

finally I call Samnang

hey he says
hey I say

you decided he says
I decided I say

well? he asks

can you come get me? I say

*now? I'm at my mother's
and I'm watching Lena and Van*

can't someone else stay with them?

he takes forever to think this over
and I have to summon all
my Japanese patience
as I wait

let me see what I can do he finally says
it may take me half an hour, okay?

finally an hour later he rings the doorbell
sticks his head inside to tell YiaYia
he'll have me home by dinner
then takes my hand

on the walkway I pause to face him
as he eyes me with anticipation

I ask if he can take me to a place
where we can see water
        if not the sea
        at least a pond
        or lake
        or river
so we can talk

there are about two hours
left of daylight

he looks toward the car
examines the sky
scrunches his face

let me call Serey he says

and I squint at him thinking
what?

for a while
he paces up and down the sidewalk
smiling, waving his hands
jabbering into his cell phone
then he returns to me

I asked her to come, too he says
and to my quizzical look
he bursts out laughing
pats my shoulder and says
kidding!
she was giving me directions

I climb into the front seat
then shriek and bump my head
at the sound of two voices
saying *hi* from the back—
Lena and Van
bundled in winter jackets

sorry, I had to bring them Samnang says

oh I say, taken aback
rubbing my head
it's fine, but . . .

I tell Samnang to wait a minute
and run back inside
grab some origami paper
and in the car I send some sheets
and a little instruction booklet
to Lena and Van in the backseat
and up front start to fold
a crane, a frog, a cicada

guys, we're going on a mystery ride
Samnang announces
to find something

golden treasure? Van asks

water says Samnang

the kids frown

the beach? Lena asks

maybe . . .

but I didn't bring my bathing suit! Van whines

it's too cold anyway Lena says

and Van scowls
shrinks down in his seat
until I toss him a frog
and its companion
cicada

on the back of a piece of origami paper
Samnang has scrawled
    495 95 113 1A
    left
    bridge
    right
    refuge
he says *hold this, in case I get lost*

soon we're out of YiaYia's neighborhood
and on the highway
but Samnang won't tell me
where we're going

mystery he says
water

when we exit
I realize we're in Newburyport
with all those big historic houses
then we turn left and suddenly
we see the mouth of the river
the one that also flows through Lowell
      and YiaYia's town
and Lena is calling out sights—
      boats in the inlet
      a tiny airfield with planes
      a bridge we cross

signs say *Plum Island*
and I vaguely recall
a day at the beach
one summer way back
with YiaYia and Papou
making a sand castle
all of us wearing long sleeves
long pants
hats
against the flies

I think I've been here I tell Samnang

the dance troupe had a beach day here
last summer he says
Serey helped organize it

at the entrance to the wildlife refuge
I pay the fee
since this outing was my idea
then Samnang parks in a lot
and we all pile out, pulling on gloves
wrapping scarves, zipping up
against the cold wind

Samnang lifts Van to his shoulders
and we walk up a boardwalk
through the grasses
and crest a dune

and suddenly we are perched
above a
not volcanic gray
but long creamy white
sand beach
at the edge
of the icy blue
Atlantic Ocean

for a moment I'm stalled
turning in both directions
holding back my whipping hair
running my tearing eyes
over and over
those far reaches of sand

and I'm thinking
as soon as she's strong enough
I'll bring my mother here

Van scrambles down
and he and Lena run toward the water
and when a wave breaks
they squeal and retreat to dry sand
Samnang takes my gloved hand
and I breathe deep the salt air

perfect I say

good he says
I figured it was my last chance

for what?

to give you a good reason to stay

I laugh
I already have plenty of reasons
but I'll add this to the list

so your decision . . .

I stop
and with my gloved hands
recessed in my jacket sleeves
turn him toward me

now who's a dodo I say
I'm staying the year, Samnang

and then I'm being kissed
and I'm in his arms
and then I'm being swung
in a circle
then dropped
right on my rear
as he goes off doing cartwheels
and back handsprings
with Lena and Van following
leaping and cartwheeling down the beach

until Van gets sand in his eyes
and cries and spits and screams
and Samnang has to wipe his face
with my scarf

when Van has recovered
Samnang starts walking
Frankenstein-style
dragging one heel
behind him
in damp sand

what are you doing? Van shouts
with his little hands on his hips

Lena and Van follow
dragging a foot each
making three parallel lines
more or less
of Samnang's writing
in the sand

when he stops
they stop
and step back to read

39? Lena says
39? Van says

and Samnang saunters over
and wraps me tight in his arms

Lena shrugs
and Van loops
from Lena to the waves
arms out, soaring
then he comes careening
and head-butts Samnang

hey! Samnang and I say
and Samnang grabs for him
and I grab for him

but Van wriggles out of reach, sprints away
and Lena laughs and starts to run with him
and Samnang and I both give chase
down the white beach
alongside the cold frothing surf

half a world away
from my other home

Poetry Mentioned in

The Language Inside

Chapter 14
"Homage to My Hips" by Lucille Clifton
"Early in the Morning" by Li Young-Li
"Introduction to Poetry" by Billy Collins

Chapter 19
"Otherwise" by Jane Kenyon
"The Legend" by Garrett Hongo

Chapter 26
"God Says Yes to Me" by Kaylin Haught
"Painting a Room" by Katia Kapovich

Chapter 33
"Mermaid Song" by Kim Addonizio
"Making a Fist" by Naomi Shihab Nye

Chapters 37 and 39
O! Maha Mount Dagrek: Poetry of Cambodian Refugee Experiences,
edited by Samkhann Khoeun

Chapter 39

"Litany for a Hidden Apsara" by Anida Yeou Ali

Chapter 41

"Enough" by Suzanne Buffam
"Running Away Together" by Maxine Kumin
"The Boundary" by Bei Dao

Chapter 44

"Patience" by Kay Ryan
"The Fist" by Derek Walcott

Recommended Resources

Books

Cambodian Dance: Celebration of the Gods by Denise Haywood
First They Killed My Father by Loung Ung
Look Up for Yes by Julia Tavalaro
Never Fall Down by Patricia McCormick
Oh Maha, Mount Dangrek, edited by Samkhann C. Khoeun
Roots and Wings by Many Ly
When Broken Glass Floats by Chanrithy Him

Films

The Diving Bell and the Butterfly, directed by Julian Schnabel
The Flute Player, directed by Jocelyn Glatzner
The Killing Fields, directed by Roland Joffé
Monkey Dance, directed by Julie Mallozzi

Websites

Angkor Dance Troupe: *angkordance.org*
Poetry Foundation: *poetryfoundation.org*
Poetry 180: *loc.gov/poetry/180/*
Poets.org: *poets.org*

Japanese Folk Dance Institute of New York: *japanesefolkdance.org*

For more resources visit Holly Thompson's website, hatbooks.com.

Acknowledgments

I am deeply grateful to Tim Thou, program director, and Linda Sopheap Sou, board president, of the Angkor Dance Troupe of Lowell, Massachusetts, and to all of the members of this phenomenal troupe, especially Emaly Horn, Virginia Prak, Sophorl Ngin, Peter Veth and Monica Veth for their guidance, patience, inspiration and encouragement during my research. I also wish to thank Sidney Liang, director of the Southeast Asian Resources for Culture and Health (SEARCH) in Lowell; Sonith Peou, director, Metta Health Center in Lowell; Dorcas Grigg-Saito, chief executive officer, Lowell Community Health Center; the Royal University of Fine Arts in Phnom Penh; Deborah Cook, RN, BSN, OCN, Oncology Patient Education Coordinator for Inova Health System Cancer Services; writers Katrina Grigg-Saito, Avery Fischer Udagawa, Suzanne Kamata and other members of SCBWI Tokyo; Pamela Thompson, my awesome ice-hockey-playing breast-cancer-survivor sister; the late poet and author Julia Tavalaro, who inspired the character of Zena; Ron Becker and Diana Cortes of the Coler-Goldwater Specialty Hospital and Nursing Facility; poet Sharon Olds and the Goldwater Writing Project; the NGO Peace Boat for the Tohoku relief and cleanup operations in which I was able to participate following the earthquake and tsunami of March 11, 2011; Julie Mallozzi for her excellent documentary *Monkey Dance*; and Heather Willson and Sovann Phon for my visits to the village of Popeae in Cambodia. I also wish to thank my ever-encouraging agent, Jamie Weiss Chilton of the Andrea Brown Literary Agency, and my ever-wise and patient editor, Françoise Bui, and all the other friends, family members, colleagues and strangers who helped this book come together. *Som or-kun. Arigato.* Thank you.

About the Author

Holly Thompson, a native of Massachusetts, is a longtime resident of Japan. She is the author of the verse novel *Orchards*, winner of the APALA Asian/Pacific American Award for Literature; the novel *Ash*; and the picture book *The Wakame Gatherers*. She is also the editor of *Tomo: Friendship Through Fiction—An Anthology of Japan Teen Stories*. Holly teaches creative writing and serves as the regional advisor for the Tokyo chapter of the Society of Children's Book Writers and Illustrators. Visit her at hatbooks.com.